Ah, but what is this *this*? And where is the usual snake-oil sell, that rearguard rodomontade designed not only to glad-hand your critical faculties but also to reassure you that having soldiered this far, you – a demanding, sophisticated, mould-breaking reader – won't be let down?

Well?

Damn good question. Just the kind one would expect from the potential owner of such a demanding, sophisticated, etc book. By way of reply, you will find fifteen stories, all rife with life in the feeder lane – stories about people who don't check the rear-view mirror before pulling away, who shift into overdrive and leadfoot it, who panic into the soft shoulder options, who, missing the warning signs, mount a noble charge on bicycles . . .

Go on. Mount a noble charge yourself. Give it a right old thumb-through. With your fellow literary lions chew over its vagaries of plot, tone and style. Check its heft by portaging it to the cash till (or if in domestic environment, slip it into a quiet pocket). JUST READ THE SUCKER. Guaranteed you will find yourself in the neighbourhood of paying attention, feet up, enjoying an unparalleled feeling of wellbeing even as the author engages his pernicious premise – to engage you even further.

Still not with me?

'David Holden has interesting things to say' – Jonathan Coe, **London Review of Books**.

Aw, shucks.

Bartender, another shot of snake-oil.

David Holden is an American writer living in London. He is a former member of the New York Herpetological Society.

THIS IS WHAT HAPPENS WHEN YOU DON'T PAY ATTENTION

DAVID HOLDEN

BLOOMSBURY

'The Onion Grass Season' first appeared in *Encounter*, November 1986;
'A Right Old Seeing-to' in *Soho Square*, November 1989;
'Americana' in *Panurge*, April 1988.

Extract from 'It Makes No Difference' by Robbie Robertson
© 1975, Medicine Hat Music, USA, reproduced by
permission of EMI Songs Ltd, London WC2H 0EA.

Bloomsbury Publishing Ltd., 2 Soho Square, London W1V 5DE

A CIP catalogue record for this book
is available from the British Library.

ISBN 0 7475 0709 0

10 9 8 7 6 5 4 3 2 1

Typeset by Hewer Text Composition Services, Edinburgh
Printed in Great Britain by Richard Clay Ltd, Bungay, Suffolk

For Mema and Bebop,
with thirty-one years of love.

CONTENTS

The Last Going-bananas at
Madhouse Mansions   1

The Onion Grass Season   15

A Right Old Seeing-to   27

Nutrasweet   37

Vive La Perspective(s)!   51

Americana   61

Headhunter Hymie Savages
Black CD Price!   79

A Barn Razing   87

Two Gallons   99

I Am Joe's Eye   107

That Motherlovin' Gauntlet   123

Once the Splinter has Worked its
Way Out, Where Does it Go?   133

Bruce 'n' Fred 'n' Gettin' Out   145

The Axolotl Grin of a Champion   171

Craving Ertia   177

The Last Going-bananas at Madhouse Mansions

I see you live in Madhouse Mansions.

What I mean is, if that place I just saw you walking out of is yours. If you live there, I mean.

Well you've got to be, in my line of work. Perceptive's the name of the game. See I'm a bond dealer in New York. Name's Phillips, how d'you do. Yeah that's right, stock market. I come through London, two, maybe three times a year on business. Get a kick out of coming back to Camden Town and re-spooking all my old haunts – but hey, you don't want to hear about me. You want to hear about Madhouse Mansions, right? Now let me just guess . . . new front hallway, something in the nice-little-varnished-pine-cheers-the-old-place-up-no-end line?

Natch. Perceptive, remember? I eat, drink and sleep perceptive. When I can get to sleep, that is. Percy Perceptive, that's me.

Incidentally what's Madhouse Mansions called these days? 'Kentish Manor Gardens' or something else suitably sane?

Mmmm. Thought so. Lovely leafy ring to it. Those scrawny little curbside saplings there really don't do it justice. Shame really your former occupants chopped up the old trees for firewood the same winter they did your hallway. I tell you, that was one cold winter – what was it, '77 or '78, I can't remember – they would've done you a favor and axed your living room too but the weather warmed up. Shame really. As I remember, that living room wasn't much to write home about either.

Yeah well, carpeting is the only recourse. You're certainly right there. Although I don't know about cream. A cream carpet wouldn't have lasted cream long in the old Madhouse Mansions.

Well, because it *was* a madhouse I guess. And it was. It was one of your quaint English breaking and entering places – a squat, yeah that's it, a squat – when I knew it, and was full of young people with no money and no furntiure but lots of dreams. Lots and lots of dreams. Some chemically induced, some not. I was a transfer student, lived around the corner in the University College dorm on Camden Road, and somebody's friend or classmate or dealer always lived in Madhouse Mansions. Plus they always threw the best parties, because they never had to worry about the place being trashed. You know? . . . It's funny – I was thinking about that just now when I looked out the window and saw you. I was thinking, 'Herb, that's the difference between then and now. Then you could live in a madhouse and go bananas and nobody cared, and now you work in one and if you go bananas, look out! You'll start another freaking Wall Street Crash.' You know? Sometimes I think they had the right . . .

. . . Sure, yeah, mine's a pint of Bass if you're buying. Thanks. I mean Cheers.

So anyway, I used to be down Madhouse Mansions a couple times a week, saying hello. Visiting. Soaking up English counterculture, like the hip transfer student I was trying hard to be. Got quite friendly with the guy and two girls in your place there, the ones responsible for the knotty-pine rethink. Was there quite a bit during term-time.

In fact I was there for the last all-out going-bananas, the one directly responsible for your sitting in this pub today. Yup. It's like I said, I'm on the verge of going bananas at work at least once a day, but it's nothing like that. I mean I could do it, I *could* start the second Wall Street Crash tomorrow and it still couldn't hold a candle to that day. Which is why I keep coming back here, going-bananas and all.

And the beer, of course. Dexter's always been a bit of an – pardon my French – A-hole, but he knows about Bass. Mud in your eye.

Mrrrahhh.

Now see that square out there? That bench? That very same bench. That's where we put the dead Arab. And it was a good thing I dropped by that day. He weighed a ton.

You know?

You want to?

I kind of thought so. Bring death into the picture and suddenly everybody's interested. Your life must be as desperate as mine, hah hah.

Well that's good to hear. Must be because the Bass is so good around here. And speaking of which, it's best to get a few rounds in now. Good hedge against the forecast decline in interest, as we say on Wall Street.

Now Bekki, Shreela and Ev – your three previous occupants – all came from the back end of Britain's beyond, some place up in the North called Bogend or Heathcliffe o' th' Moors or something like that. They came along with all the others in that great mid-'70s trudge down to London. You know the scene – everybody flat broke and looking for fame and fortune. And work. Well Bekki was anyway. Shreela was looking for a more stimulating environment to defraud the welfare state in. And Ev – he just came along for the heck of it. With his fiddle under his chin, as he always did.

By the time I got to know them they'd been in Madhouse Mansions almost a year. Bekki was waitressing and trying to make it as a punk singer, screeching in an endless series of bands with names like Coitus Interruptus, Siamese Hitler Twins, The Four Asterisks – each a little worse and a lot louder than the one before. In fact, when she was one of The Four Asterisks Dexter did them a favor and booked them into the function room upstairs, but then threw them out after the vibration from their first number broke all the glasses on his back bar. Very punk. But even more punk was Bekki's hair – truly amazing, like she hadn't ducked low enough going under a rainbow. Used to make money by going down the King's Road Saturday mornings and charging tourists a pound for a shot of An Authentic Punk Rocker. Which is the closest she ever got to being it.

Mrrrahhh.

Shreela, she was a different ball of wax altogether. She's probably a millionaire by now. In fact, now that I think of it she'd make a great broker. You see, on the bus down from the North she'd found Shreela E. Ghosh's wallet and with a little market awareness was able to make a killing claiming both her own and Shreela E.'s social security benefits.

No, I don't have the slightest how. But she did.

Bullish, we call it on Wall Street. The makings of a great broker. She spent a lot of time in the outskirts of London, buying on credit, opening bank accounts and the like, all in Shreela E.'s name. She also did a sideline in certain substances we called study aids – helped her with accumulating capital and kept the rest of us going during those all-night cram sessions.

No, I don't think she was Indian. Or Pakistani. But then again, she wasn't exactly peaches and cream either. Tell you the truth I don't know what she was. Apart from bullish.

Ev, now there was a classic odd man out. In every sense. His kind comes along only once in your lifetime. There simply isn't enough conceivability for more than that, let me tell you. On nice days he accompanied the girls out on their Camden Town forages, helping them sift through the newly gentrified areas' dumpsters for furniture and firewood. Most of the time though, while Bekki was out working or singing and

Shreela out defrauding or dealing, he just stayed at Madhouse Mansions and played his violin. If it was warm out, as you passed you could hear his Telemann or Vivaldi wafting over everybody else's Sex Pistols or Clash.

And a rare sound it was too. His genius for classical music was something appreciable even to hardened Sex Pistols fans. And the way he played – unfiltered Woodbine rammed in his mouth, enormous flitting fingers drifting down onto the violin neck like leaves, then suddenly touching off a note or a run like unexpected sparks from a dying fire – it gave you a feeling. A tingling twinge back of your head – here, right about here. Feel that? God, it was amazing. I've never felt anything like it. Ever.

And I don't even like violins much.

Ev had that ability of all geniuses to make people want to do things for them, nurture and protect them, say, 'Kid, I'm gonna make you a star.' Nobody more so than Bekki and Shreela. They'd come home from a hard day's waitressing or fraud or whatever with nothing more than a few frozen dinners, the rest of the food money blown on resin or strings from Guivier's in Mortimer Street, the only store Ev knew in London. It never bothered them, at least it never seemed to, that he didn't try to exploit his talent – you know, earn a few bucks playing in an orchestra or one of those string quartets, or even just busking around West End tube stations. Lord knows they could've used the money. To buy things like a new hallway for example. But you see, doing things for money was just as alien to Ev as not doing them for money was to the girls. He used to tell me playing the violin was his way of connecting – himself to himself, himself to music, himself to others. That those others would then take care of life's mundanities seemed to be built into the deal.

Great way to live, huh?

You know, day before I came to London I had to go to my orthodontist and get fitted for a second one of these. Here. Look at this. See, it's a plate I have to wear every night to keep my teeth from grinding together in my sleep. I bit through the first one last week. Stress, the ortho says. Equivalent of two hundred pounds of pressure per square inch.

Two hundred pounds per square inch.

So anyway, for about a year those three were the happiest household in Madhouse Mansions. In their unofficial careers they managed as much contentment as anyone could – drove Dexter crazy running up enormous tabs, marked the passing of time in hair dye, final demands and bowstrings – and in their official ones scraped by as Unemployment Figures.

Until the day Bekki caught the eye of the Arab.

Now is an excellent time to get in another round.

Now before – I'm keeping track of all these, you know – before we go into any gory details, you should know a few additional things about Ev. First of all, his name. As you probably already guessed with Shreela, what everybody called him wasn't really who he was. For survival's sake most Madhouse Mansions inmates had pseudonyms – kept all the messy paperwork in places like social security offices and police stations out of their hair. Now for all I know Ev's name *might* have been Evan or even, God help him, Evelyn, but whenever a proper name was mentioned in context it was always Everest.

Yeah, that's right. Like the one in China.

Wherever. On account of his size you see. In Britain, if you'll pardon me a country not exactly known for man-mountains, Ev was freakin' Himalayan. Big height, big hands, big feet, big gut courtesy of his other love, Tim Taylor's Championship Beers, Ev would stand in the doorway of his flat like a big old chuckwalla wedged in a crevice, and if his attention was distracted you'd have to go all the way around the back and in through the coal scuttle. Drunks in the pubs up North used to play what we in the States call chicken – you know, 'beshya nex' round ya wone go up 'n' take a poke at 'im' – using Ev as the target. But far back as anyone could remember Ev'd never actually taken part in a fight, partly because most people gave up when they discovered how hard they'd have to try to inflict any damage.

And partly because he couldn't see a fight coming if it busted a bar-stool over his head. I mean you and me, we're the type been scrapping since practically the day we were born – yeah, now you got it, perceptive – and we know when something's gonna happen. Whether we're gonna get murdered, whether we can take the guy, that sort of thing. Male instinct, you know.

But Ev, I don't know, he was like some kind of throwback. One of those enormous Brontosaurus-type things, not stupid but placid, which somehow slipped through an evolutionary loophole. I don't know, maybe it was his chromosomes or something – but then again it couldn't be because he loved women. Lived with two of 'em, had just about all the ones he knew eating out of his hand. Fell in love about once a day. I remember walking down Royal College Street out there with him and some little *chiquita* on her way to North London Poly sashaying by and that would be it for Ev. You ever gone, wha-da-ya-call-it-here walkies with a Great Dane? You go where they want to go. Same with Ev. I'd have to chase after him, pull him off, apologize – but he always came away with a phone number. Because for some dark mysterious shrouded-in-the-mists-of-Time reason women all loved him back.

Truth.

Mrrahhh. What I wouldn't give to know his secret. Could use a *chiquita* myself right around now.

Search me. I guess if an enormous strong macho guy maybe like in the movies can make women swoon, maybe the opposite is true – an enormous strong non-macho one can make them swoon too. Like maybe it's just as sexy or whatever to have all that power and not display it as it is *to* display it. Except I don't think Ev even knew he had it in the first place. Maybe *that's* sexy.

Maybe he just had a massive wang.

Ah Christ, if we sit here and spend our time trying to figure out why he got laid and I didn't all we'll get is drunk. Very, very drunk. And old Ev'll never get to take care of this Arab.

So anyway, he really pulled the birds, as you Brits say. Whole flocks of 'em, Bekki and Shreela included. And one more thing: no fights ever. Among any of them. He must've spread the lotion around mighty thinly but it seemed to keep them all happy. I got this mental image of Ev and his women — like he was sitting on a gigantic powder keg smoking a Woodbine and lacking a few scientific facts. But nothing happened, nobody ever exploded. Nobody went bananas. And Ev just carried on, fiddle under his chin; men kept their distance and women didn't.

Until, as you no doubt guessed, the Arab.

Yes the bloody Arab again.

No listen it's my round, I really ought . . . OK. I just don't want you to think I'm spinning some yarn to soak you for beer or something.

Yeah, Bass is fine. Make sure freakin' Dexter tops it up. He's an A-hole like that.

So Bekki lands this waitressing job. In one of those kitschy pseudo-American burger joints in Earls Court. Called Memorabilia I think it was, all fake '50s junk and food likewise. What is it Bekki used to call it . . . Memorabilious. She was a great one for puns, that Bekki. Yep.

Tipping at Memorabilious was at the customer's discretion, which for waitresses in this country is usually the kiss of death — hey, no offence, you strike me as at least a twelve percenter — but the clientele in Memorabilious was mainly us Yanks and Arabs, so she usually made out OK. Yanks she used to say tipped big to impress each other, Arabs to impress the waitress. And so it happened one night she got this humongous tip from this table of Arabs, all in traditional get-up, who'd been gorging themselves all night on Drive-In Style Chicken Wings or some such crap. And when she got off work late that night there they were again, in true Earls Court fashion double-parked in a black Mercedes right out front of the restaurant.

Mrrrahhh.

It was her hairstyle I think really was her undoing. I guess the women back in Saudi Arabia or wherever don't go around with rainbow-colored hair, least the wives of the Arabs I do business with don't. Anyway, according to Bekki, the conversation centered on her hair, the color of it, and would she be willing – for a small fee of course – to show it to a few friends at some casino in Knightsbridge. Paid escort sort of thing, you catch my drift? Now as we've discussed a) Bekki was no dope and b) she was not averse to squeezing the odd pound out of the way she looked, but on her own terms. And jumping into a strange car with a load of Bar-B-Q burping Bahrainis didn't exactly constitute her own terms. Can you blame her? So she very politely thanks 'em and jumps on a passing night bus to Camden.

Picture this: it's very early on a dull Wednesday morning; the casinos suddenly seem even duller; the Arabs decide to tail her. A bottle of Johnnie Walker Red gets an airing and warms 'em all the way to Chalk Farm Road.

And the going-bananas business begins.

Bekki gets off the bus in Camden Town and's almost home free, right, in fact she could hear Ev attacking a particularly finger-snarling bit of a Bach partita she'd bought, when the Mercedes slides up. And out stumbles one of the Arabs, the one who suggested she come to the casino, much the worse for wear, and he goes to drag her into the back seat.

Yeah I know, but it's not just them – I saw a broker type try it once down South Street in New York. Nah, she was all right. Knew kung fu or something. Whack, straight to the family jewels. Walked a bit wobbly myself after seeing that.

So anyway, Bekki screams and kicks and punches and manages to free herself long enough to sprint the hundred yards or so to the flat. She tears up the steps and as the Arab staggers up the street after her, shakily dials the combination lock on the front door. She throws the door open and clears the floor joins of the hallway OK in one gigantic leap and lands, still screaming, on the living room floor.

Ev and Shreela are there, bug-eyed. 'There's a man,' Bekki goes, 'after me . . . Customer . . . Arab.' Then they hear the sound of the Arab lurching up the front steps, planning to storm the hallway and sweep Bekki off to some harem somewhere, or something. Then they hear the crash.

And what a fucking crash.

Shreela looks at Ev. And he's shaking almost bad as Bekki. So she takes over, like usual. 'I'll take Bekki out the back and call the police from the call-box in the square,' she goes.

Bekki wails, 'It's not working!'

Shreela goes, 'We'll find one that is. Gimme all your two ps.' Ev turns out his pockets and there's Shreela picking through 'em like a gull on a garbage dump. 'That'll do,' she goes. She helps Bekki up. Out in the hall they can hear the Arab moaning and picking himself up.

'I'll give Johnny and Spike next door a shout on the way out,' she calls as she shoves Bekki out the back way, 'you take care of the Arab.'

By now Ev's trembling's reached seismic proportions. 'What'll I do?' he whispers. His violin slips away, clatters on the floor.

Shreela's reply was impatient, a grinding reminder of how things in the real world are – three words at two hundred pounds per square inch: 'You're the man.'

This pint's not as good as the others, lookit all that sediment. Lookit. Dexter's been tampering with his beer. Take it back and tell him he's an A-hole. A first-rate fart factory. Tell 'im.

Now just hang on, let me finish this first.

A few seconds later the Arab's sort of regained control and managed to half-crawl, half-stumble into the living room. He's panting and sweating and moaning Bekki's name in a drunk guttural voice. He looks up and there's Ev climbing out the window.

'You Bekki boyfriend?' he hiccupped, drunk-like.

Ev turned almost apologetically, looked at the Arab. The Arab looked at Ev. Then Ev wiped his hands on his jeans, chewed his lips awhile, stepped back into the room. He went over to the Arab. He put his arms around him and held him tight.

And tighter.

And tighter, like a python. And as the Arab's tremblings increased Ev felt his own decreasing until he was completely still. A strange sort of inner peace. Told me later he liked it. Like Bach's first concerto for violin and harpsichord.

And then the Arab was still too. And Ev realized with horror it was all over.

He was indeed the man.

Now it just so happens – now this one looks a lot better, didja tell him, no I didn't think ya would – it just so happens I was up pulling an all-nighter for a pathetically put-off paper on Spenser, the Elizabethan tradition and any other sixteenth-century bullshit could flesh it out to 10,000 words, and decided to go around to Shreela to see what sort of study aids were on offer.

Come to think of it, nowadays she wouldn't even hafta be a broker – could just carry on dealing study aids. Hers were certainly higher grade than any around New York today I can tell you, and she was a helluva more pleasant than somebody I know . . .

When I saw a light on in the living room I figure I'm in luck, OK?

No chance. Ev was in, as you say over here, a state. Seriously going bananas. He's thrown the Arab over his shoulder like a bedroll and's traipsing around the room in circles looking like fucking Baden-Powell deciding where to pitch camp. Johnny and Spike were there too, but they'd just come back from a gig and were on something and just stood there in the doorway wild-eyed.

Mrrrrrrrrrrrrrrrrraaaaaaaaaaaaaahhhhhhhhhhhhhhhhhhhh.

Enter me, ya know? And I don't know the Arab's dead, I don't know the Arab from fucking Mohammed, I just saw him and Ev going around and around and Johnny and Spike gawping at them, and I think I made some crack about, hey what was this, has Ev finally gotten into professional wrestling, and then I saw the Arab's face.

And I knew then.

Ah – empty.

Next.

Shreela came back a few minutes later to say all the fucking phones were broken and she'd left Bekki with some friends to calm down. I was in their cluttered kitchen trying to scare up some cups for tea. Feeling a lot cluttered myself.

I mean, like the guy's dead, right?

She went past me into the living room and found out for herself. I heard her crying for a bit, only time I ever knew she did. When I come back in Ev's just dumped the Arab on the floor and he and Shreela're in a corner of the room, holding each other like two pioneers who've just lost everything in an Apache attack.

Johnny and Spike musta been coming down because all of a sudden they start asking questions.

So there we all are sitting in Madhouse Mansions – the two Northerners, the two druggies and the two foreigners – and suddenly Spike points out the Arab musta been with friends who're probably wondering. And we all think, shit! and find the empty bottle of Johnnie Walker on him and decide to carry him over the square and dump him on a bench and make it look like he just passed out from drinking. Another case of excessive Western indulgence sorta thing.

So off we go. Shreela and me did most of the carrying – Ev didn't want to touch the body and Spike and Johnny claimed to be still too spaced out. I never carried someone dead before but it's amazing how unaffected you can be when it's someone not only dressed different, but you don't even know. He felt like a couple months of dirty laundry.

Next.

*

12

We got him to that bench, *that bench right there*, that one, propped him up, folded his arms around the bottle and left him looking for all the world like he'd been shown one helluva time at Madhouse Mansions.

And about a half hour later and the sun's just beginning to come up and we're all drinking two-handed cups of tea like fucking geriatrics with the shakes, and Bekki comes in. She'd calmed down a lot on her way back until she saw the Mercedes again, at the square. Managed to keep from screaming and hid behind some garbage cans. Watched it circle the square twice, like a shark homing in on its prey. Then it stops and these two Arabs jump out, look around guiltily and bundle our Arab into the back seat. Then it roars off, laying wheels that stayed there for weeks.

Bekki tells us all this and we just held our breath and took up battle stations. Except her and Ev, who get sent to the kitchen to be out of harm's way. When we finally relaxed about an hour later we found them asleep under the fucking kitchen table, wrapped up together like two runaways. Bekki sighed, Johnny and Spike invited me back to check out some of their study aids, and that pretty much was that.

Until two weeks later Camden fuckin' Council suddenly chucked everybody out. Relocated, in their words – shipped 'em all off to nightmare estates in some north London hellhole somewhere. Boarded up Madhouse Mansions and eventually sold it to whoever sold it to you. Course I was gone by then, back in the States taking a load of shit from my old man for wanting to do my Master's at Oxford instead of entering his old brokerage house. I never saw Bekki or Shreela or Ev or a textbook again.

Next.

Nah, didn't think ya would. Truth being stranger 'n fiction an' all that. And of course you as the incumbent, ya know? Who wantsta know they're livin' in a place been stained by death?

No, hey – sorry. Didn' mean it. Didn'. It's just that those times, like I didn' know it at the time, but they were outa ordinary. I thought everytime was gonna be bananas, a rush, mem'ry like that. Not that I condone death or anythin', jus' these days ya know, ortho plates. Ortho fuckin' plates.

Funny, I think 'bout those three mostly when I'm at work. Specially Ev. An' y'know, I can't 'magine him alive today. How he'd fit in. Young people, that age everybody got so much patience, nobody breathin' down their neck.

An' I can't bear to 'magine him dead but . . .

Lissen. Lissen, I got'n idea – I gotta catch the redeye ta New York in two hours – get me there seven a.m. for meetin' at nine. Boss says future of my department's ridin' on it. Let's you an' me go bananas here for the nex' two hours an' see wha' happens, hey? I probly owe you 'bout a million drinks anyway . . . Whadja say? Hah? In mem'rya Madhouse Mansions . . . ja feel like just goin' bananas?

Mrrraaahhh.

The Onion Grass
Season

*Too cruel to some is the rushing shriek of Being – they
cannot stand the world.*
M. P. Shiel, The House of Sounds

Whitney Grey Turner was absolutely furious with his wife,
who had died the day before. He sat on the edge of the bed
they had shared for forty-six years and lit a cigarette. It was
his first in five years.

It amazed him how quickly all his old smoking habits
returned – the two quick taps on the bottom of the pack
to coax out the first cigarette, the rolling motion between
the fingers to check for defects, the bull's-eye stab to the
centre of the mouth which preceded lighting up. He huddled
over and around the cigarette. Even though he was indoors
he cupped the lit match in his hands. The flame leaped up
angrily, flagged, then went out. He lit another and brought it
to the tip. The smoke seeped between the gaps in his teeth and
twined itself around his tonsils. He swallowed and shuddered
slightly. He shook out the match and stared hostilely at her
side of the bed.

('Emphysema,' he told her when he got back from the hospital. 'Doctor says quit smoking starting today if I want to see tomorrow.' He hung up his coat. She nodded slowly, deliberately, shaking off the unthinkable. 'We'll stop today, Whit,' she said, taking his arm in hers and stroking the deep veiny valleys between his knuckles with her smooth white fingers. 'We'll stop today.')

He exhaled the smoke with a snort. Damn Camilla, she was always like that. Damn his dead wife. You know she never smoked a day in her life. Hardly ever took a drink either, except maybe holidays and the odd social occasion. But that day he had come home from the hospital there she was, all ready to take the blame for it. All ready to share his penance. Damn his dead wife! *His* emphysema, *his* clogged lungs, *his* going cold turkey, *his* last few years tarnished when they should be golden, and she had wanted to share it! He remembered wanting to line up a whole pack of cigarettes between his lips, light them all at once, and inhale himself to death. After all he was seventy-five then; he was not going to see his life out a cripple. But Camilla, goddamn Camilla who wouldn't know which end to light, had taken his arm and said, 'We'll stop today.' And they had. And now yesterday she'd stopped everything else.

He smoked fiercely, puffing two, three, four times before he exhaled. The smoke belched from his nose and mouth like dark smog, wreathing him in angry pollution. From within the cigarette flicked up and down in a pistoning motion.

('He liked the X-rays,' he said, hanging up his coat. He watched the deep wrinkles in her face subside into the much lighter and more agreeable ones of age. He smoothed the more stubborn with his thumb and whisked away a small tear cowering in the corner of her eye. 'He says of course the emphysema's no better than when I was smoking, but in the six months since I quit there's been no increase.'

'That's very, very good, Whit,' she said evenly. She managed a smile and told him his favorite dinner was in the oven.)

16

The cigarette was almost finished. He picked it out of his mouth and held it between his thumb and forefinger. When they first met he always held his cigarette that way. But he stopped when Camilla said she didn't like it. Said it made him look unsavory, as if he should be leaning up against a sweaty lamppost in a red-light district. He preferred to think it made him look heroic, like one of the GIs in those old combat movies. Snatching the last drag between thumb and finger before taking that hill. For a second the bedroom vanished and he was in the trenches – joking nervously with the boys, wondering what was on the other side, blowing smoke-rings into the battle-weary air. Then somebody gave a signal. Half-smoked butts went arcing across the front, and he was left behind again. He got up stiffly and stared at the bed. He felt his anger detonating in him. God *damn* his dead wife! What right did she have to go off to the other side now, now when he really needed her, now when he could finally do as he liked? How dare she! He stabbed the cigarette out savagely in the sheets on her side of the bed. It left a dark smoldering gash. Wisps of smoke, tainted with the springtime scent of the fabric softener Camilla used in the laundry, rose to his nostrils. He put his fists to his temples and went out of the room.

Quiet. Quiet. Quiet. He hadn't heard so much quiet in all his life. It was much louder than the quiet of the library fifty years ago where he studied for his Bar exams. It was far more clamorous than the quiet forty-five years ago when the doctor padded out of the hospital room to tell him he was very sorry but the baby was not born alive. More thunderous than the quiet which had roared through his brain as he stood there, inanely wondering why the doctor had said 'not born alive' instead of 'born dead'. More deafening than the quiet which hung over their bed for two years, until Camilla finally allowed him to try again to make a family. This quiet now was the sum total of all that quiet plus more: the pallor of death, the calmness of resting, the dust-gathering of inactivity. The Horse Latitudes of a widower's life. It was insidious and addictive: it drew him into it, made him lean attentively forward in his chair, creep around the house softly and stealthily so as not to disturb it. He stopped often on his rounds, listening keenly for the sound of Camilla in the kitchen or his own voice bellowing from the bedroom about the whereabouts of his brown socks. He would just about hear them, be that first decibel away from breaking the quiet down with a response, his own voice a potential strident horn in the morgue-like Jericho of his house – then his common sense would come to the rescue. 'You're imagining things,' it would say, 'come on, get a grip on yourself.' And being a lawyer, a man of practical outlook, he would, and sit back down and light a cigarette.

'Come on, Dad. I know how you feel, but you've got to come to the funeral.' His son, the successful product of that attempt forty-three years ago, looked strained.

'No.'

'You're making this hard on all of us.'

'I don't care.'

His son didn't respond, just looked disgustedly away as his father reached for another cigarette. Charles Hodgson Turner got out of his chair with a grunt, the kind of grunt his father would never admit to. A grunt signalling that age was starting to call in all bets. Charles wandered over to the window. He moved with the same gait he used whenever the arbitration talks he mediated for a living broke down: a stoop-shouldered loping shuffle, hands jammed in pockets, designed to illustrate both the strain he was being put under and his dogged perseverance. He sighed.

He watched his father, reflected in the window glass and unaware of his scrutiny. His father at eighty could easily pass for a man of sixty-five. His hair, although thin, still covered his head in a swatch of untinted brown. It condescended to grey only at his temples. His mother used to complain boastfully about this on their trips to Florida. She always came back with lurid stories about fending eligible widows off him with a shuffleboard cue. His father would laugh lightly, shaking his head at his wife's over-active imagination.

Throughout the years his father's face, instead of seizing up with wrinkles, had gone slack and jowly. This left him with smooth, almost cherubic features. His cheeks were rouged with a network of minuscule crisscrossing veins. The only concession to eighty years of living was a discolored wrinkled flap of loose skin under his chin. Looking at him now, Charles fancied that that must be where his father hid his share of the ravages of time: like paint thrown on glass everything had slid down his face and collected underneath. But even that dewlap befriended him – it fluttered and wriggled like a puppy's tail, every bit as uncontrollable, imparting an air of youthful waggishness every time he spoke.

Which was why it was so damn hard trying to reason – or argue – with him. Without even knowing it he made you like him, want to agree with him. Simply because of that thing dangling from his chin – it was so damn entertaining. Charles stared at it mesmerized, thankful that he'd never come up against it in arbitration. It seemed to stretch straight out at him, beckoning, then snapped back as his father spoke.

'We had an arrangement, you know – when we were married. We made a deal. And now she's gone back on it.' Turner spoke curtly, through chimneys of smoke. Charles turned away from the window.

'What do you mean, an arrangement? A wedding licence?'

'No,' his father snapped.

'Well, what? A dowry?'

The dewlap rippled as his father snorted. 'I may be old-fashioned, Charlie, but I'm not that old-fashioned.' The dewlap was still. His father smoked quietly.

Charles was beginning to lose his patience. 'She'd die if she saw you doing that,' he said abruptly, realizing too late his mistake. How could he, an arbitration lawyer, have been that tactless?

The dewlap was motionless but he heard his father's voice, far away and bitter: 'She died because I wasn't doing that.'

His training told Charles to ignore that comment. Pass it off as something said in the heat of the moment and get back to the bargaining table. But something filial in him made him want to probe. To get to the bottom of these two people who had spent almost half a century together and whose unforeseen separation was bringing out such hostility in his father. These two totally disparate natures who had kept a forty-six-year vow of consummate coexistence, including losing a daughter and raising a son.

'Now what's that supposed to mean?' Charles tried to sound offhand and uninterested.

'We ran out of things to share. We got old. Kids went, friends died – only thing we had for company was our goddamn diseases. And dying. So the doctors take away the diseases, and now *she* takes away the other.'

'Dying?'

'Yep.' His dewlap shook as if an earthquake had hit it.

'And that's why you won't go to the funeral? Because you're frigging *mad* at her?'

His father said nothing but his dewlap stirred.

('You are my wife.' He said it almost with glee. In his thirty-five years he had never known glee. Or dizzying happiness for that matter, or rock-solid satisfaction or supercharged anticipation. Or love. Or any of the countless sensations currently electrifying the space between the sheets, crackling the air around himself and his bride of seven hours.

'I am your wife.' She said it with the seriousness of a woman much older. She was nineteen. 'Camilla Millicent Dodgson Turner.'

'Mrs Whitney Grey Turner, if you please.' He turned over on his side and put his hand gently around her tiny waist.

'Mrs Whitney Grey Turner. Wife of the famous lawyer.'

'Almost famous.' His hand moved up her nightdress, found the gap of the neckline and slipped in. She shuddered slightly, not from stimulation or fear, but because she was thinking hard about her future as Mrs Whitney Grey Turner.

He brought his mouth over to join his hand, and while one explored the limits of the fabric the other clambered up her breastbone, testing her skin with small flicks of the tongue. She tasted fresh and dewy. His tongue darted in and out of the deep hollows at the base of her neck, tasting.

She was still thinking. Who was this man she had married? He was gentle, immodestly gentle her body was telling her, but was his gentleness a natural outpouring of his soul or simply a means to bind the two of them forever tighter together?

'You have done a very selfish thing,' she said.

He appeared not to listen, to be too caught up in plumbing the nape of her neck. She tugged at his long, loose chin.

'You have married a woman fifteen years younger than you, knowing full well you will probably die first and leave her alone for the rest of her life.'

His head came up incredulously from her neck – this was their wedding night!

'But it's all right,' she continued, 'it's all right because I love you and want to share the rest of your life with you. Regardless of how long or short it is. That's what I was put here for. To be with you.'

He looked at her for a long time; this was their wedding night.)

That was the arrangement. And yesterday she reneged on it. From the window Turner watched the confused exasperated way his son maneuvered the car in his narrow driveway. It shot off in a splatter of gravel. Then the quiet descended again.

While Charles was booming out 'Ahhhhh-men' to one of his mother's favorite hymns his father was just around the corner, walking. He was in the park where he and Camilla had courted forty-seven years ago. But he wasn't thinking about

Camilla because he wasn't smoking – he tended to think of her most fervidly while the tobacco was screeching through his lungs. Right now since she was no longer alive the lawyer, the man of practical outlook, did not think about her.

Instead he concentrated on an overview of the thirty-five years before she came. He had spent most of that time alone – though not necessarily lonely. Loneliness lives in flights of melancholic fancy; aloneness accepts the existence of a few basic facts. He had slowly, falteringly, become acquainted with aloneness as an only child; explored its solitude and solidity as a shy, ungregarious adolescent; and unable (or unwilling, he didn't know which) to turn his back on it as an adult had grudgingly made room for it among his legal briefs and Bar association dinners. And now at the very end of his life, after he had kicked it out to make room for Camilla, that aloneness returned. It took over the spot she had vacated. And padding behind it came the quiet, descended from the loathsome quiet of his childhood, which right now howled in his ears. The man of practical outlook was deafened.

Turner felt something catch his foot. He had to stumble forward to avoid falling. He swore and looked down. A raised clump of onion grass bore the imprint of his shoe. He swore again and noticed that the entire stretch of park before him was sporting the same growth. It was the onion grass season: clumps of rigid green dotted the landscape like grown-out crew cuts. Next to some were gouged neat round pockmarks. Children had yanked up patches of grass to hurl at the sky and watch captivated as they streamed meteor-like back to earth. The simplicity of the act made Turner envious; the child's unreasoned joy of throwing something into the air.

His envy vanished as he recalled his own childhood. He had done the very same thing at the boarding schools his parents sent him to: a lone child in an empty playing field, tossing his time away. Playing catch with the sun and a ball of onion grass as quiet, not his mother, looked on. He stamped through the park, seeking out and trampling clumps. And then as a young man, parents separated, mother dead, taking long walks alone to shatter the silence of study – academic quiet replaced by alfresco quiet. More clumps flattened underfoot, scrunching as the roots and bulbs crushed against his soles. But all the noise of then and now dinning inside his head, the eternal shriek and skree of facts, figures and feelings! – sometimes he thought his mind would explode. And one day years too late, long after he had given up sandbagging himself with onion grass games and walks outdoors, he met Camilla. And for forty-six years the explosive fuse spluttered only intermittently, dampened by her liquid love.

He came to the bridge which crossed the park pond. After some hesitation he started across it. It wasn't the same bridge he knew in his courting days; that one had been a rickety wooden structure splayed across the water on knobbly pilings. From a distance it always reminded him of an old lady with her skirts hiked up wading across. The new bridge was a replacement, put in a few years ago when vandals burned the old bridge down. It was a typical County Parks Commission bridge – solid no-nonsense concrete thrusting directly from one side to the other. Turner stopped in the middle of it. He looked at everything except the water.

('Whit, I know how much you hate scenes, so I won't make one.' She watched him staring at her from the end of the bed. His eyes blinked rapidly and his dewlap twitched. 'Whit, I don't want to make it through the night.' Her voice came to him in a tunnel, rattling hollowly. The heart attack, although sparing her life, had killed her lust for it; *vita* [his law-school Latin came back to him] without vitality. 'I feel like everything's been switched off and I can't switch it back on.' Her head sank into the bank of pillows. 'I don't even know if I want to.' She looked at him blinking and twitching. 'Whitney – I love you and I've loved only you for the last forty-six years.' She lifted her head a bit. 'Did you know it was forty-six years?' He snorted tentatively. 'Of course I knew.' She settled back in the pillows. 'Liar.' Then she didn't speak for a long time.

When she spoke next her voice sounded run-down. Her

breath came in heaves. He knew she was speaking to him through another attack, a much smaller one this time, and he took her frail fingers in his. What else to do when the only one to bring humanity to your life is about to leave it? 'Imagine,' she whispered, 'imagine you outliving me, Whit.' A flicker of a smile – or maybe it was a grimace – played across her face. Her wrinkles had doubled in the last hour, it seemed. Her face was a mass of convolusions, swallowing up any expression. She looked suddenly much older than her sixty-five years. 'Sorry,' she rasped.

'Sorry,' he echoed. 'Don't be sorry, Camilla.' He tried to smooth her wrinkles but they wouldn't be budged, felt like topography under his fingers. 'Please don't be sorry.' He spoke soothingly, as though she were the daughter he never knew. He felt her grip loosening. 'Don't be sorry, Cammy, Cammy – ' he hadn't called her that since their courting days. Her eyelids flickered recognition of the distant past. 'Cammy, listen to me, listen – ' one hand gripped hers tighter, the other went under the bedclothes and around her still tiny waist, ' – I waited thirty-five years for you once, I can wait a few more for you again – '

'Again forever,' she breathed. And then just like in those old combat movies his greatest comrade, his truest friend died in his arms.)

He was smoking on the bridge now, cigarette wedged between thumb and forefinger. It was growing dark; the service was probably over. His son would be on his way to the house soon, to arbitrate with him some more. To hell with his son. To hell with his dead wife. They were nothing but obstructions anyway, roadblocks put up to divert him from a few basic facts: he entered this world solo; was going to exit it solo; now was the time to get to know that feeling and get to know it good. What had Camilla done but distract him from these facts for most of his life, only to bail out right when he thought the two of them together had them licked? How could she have loved him so with one breath and then left him so alone by not taking the next? Camilla Camilla Camilla Camilla come back come back come back come back come back – this would not do. The man of practical outlook took charge. He finished his cigarette, sent it over the railing, and followed it.

He sank deep into the belly of the pond and waited for an ending. None came. Finally the roar of the quiet, amplified in water, became too much. Like a turtle coming out of hibernation, dewlap stretched almost to snapping, he craned his head out of the ooze. He started to move. He struck out for shore, half-hoping it wouldn't be there. His sodden clothes dragged him down. Then the pain began in his side and he remembered: he was an old sick man and old sick men don't go swimming. The pain raced the length of his body. He felt as if he was swimming in a pool of hardening concrete. Every scoop of water, every limp kick was like rubbing himself up against a rock. Yet his heart beat on, his eyes told him the shoreline was not far away. He groped and floundered and got closer.

But never quite all the way there, because he realized as he started to sink he was destined never to get all the way there. He would never totally get to know that aloneness, that feeling, not through anybody else, not even by himself. Those basic facts remained as obvious and elusive as the universe.

The pain increased. The pond grew larger. The onion grass on the nearby shore swayed and danced in the evening breeze like sea anemones.

A Right Old
Seeing-to

It is there first thing in the morning, a bloodstained banner of conquest flapping from his mother's clothesline. I see it from the Lucknow kitchen and think: so much blood. Did he see-to Michelle or kill her? In this neighborhood neither is ever out of the question. Especially after a night down the pub.

I turn to tell the guv'nor Kevin. He sits at the kitchen table ploughing through a bowl of overmilked cornflakes, eyes nailed to the *News of the World*.

'Gazza's gone and done the dirty deed. Just like he said he would last night. Given her a right old seeing-to.'

'Aye, I couldn't help but see it. It's right outside my fuckin' window.' He grins through a mouthful of sogginess. 'His mother'll kill him when she sees. Fuckin' kill him she will.'

'No doubt.'

'Just as long as we don't have to clean up the mess, eh Jim?' He gets up, sighs, scratches his belly, puts the bowl in the sink. I nod. He pulls aside the grimy net curtains and peers out. 'I'm tellin' you, Jim, these people are no better than animals. We're supposed to be the animals, they're supposed to be the fuckin' Empire.' He lets the curtain drop.

He says that to their faces often, especially after they've had a few and are pounding on the bar for more. But even then Gaz and his crew consider Kevin an all-right bloke, because sometimes he deigns to buy a round. And when he does it's like a condensed Guy Fawkes party – laughing, shouting, displays, and, most of all, singing. They all join hands around the guv'nor, stare weavily into his fiery eyes, and give him a good Oirish song – 'Danny Boy', the only one they know. Because he's an all-right bloke, and because he can hear the till trilling like a frantic xylophone, Kevin lets them carry on for a good hour past closing. Then it's all business. 'Oh Kevvie boy, the pipes're callin' the last one wails as he's steered firmly beyond the pale. The guv'nor slides the bolt home with a crack like a rifle loading. 'Fuckin' animals.'

At eleven o'clock I am behind the bar and at exactly eleven-fifteen, same as every day, Gaz is on the other side. He places his usual order in his usual tone, my personal swaggering Westminster chimes, 'Pint of lager-top, mate.' While I get it for him he drums on the counter top and looks out the front door, the one facing the tower blocks of Dickens Estate. He is waiting for one of his mates to arrive so he may commence the saga of the seeing-to. I push his pint across the bar. 'One pound thirty-five.' He pays without taking his eyes off the door. His fingers drum frantically. He is bursting to tell someone.

He won't tell me though. Because I don't exist. I am not a human being; I am an extension of the bar counter, a dispensing machine. In the rigidly defined Dickens Estate caste system bums and bartenders (particularly foreign ones) are at the bottom. I am an Untouchable, a victim of both my New Jersey upbringing and my ignorance of day-to-day Dickens Estate affairs. However, today I could improve my lot. I have seen the evidence.

Today is a good day – we both hear the door handle jiggle not long after Gaz is served. Some days Gaz has to wait fifteen, twenty minutes before one of his crew arrives; I've watched him wait, beer untouched, for half an hour before the handle jiggles. Whereupon it's, 'While you're at it get Terry a drink', as though he's just arrived himself, on his way to something much more important. I always cover for him wordlessly; as an Untouchable I enjoy a certain omniscience – accepted by my betters as long as it's mute.

Today it is not Terry but his younger brother, Davey. At twenty Davey is five years less a man of the world than Gaz. But he is eager to learn, which is why he is usually the second person in the pub. He is a barrow boy and works for Gaz's father selling fruit and vegetables by the touristy tube stations near Dickens Estate – Covent Garden, Russell Square and Holborn. So far his eagerness has stood him in good stead; recently he was given his own pitch around the side of Holborn.

It was the promotion Gaz would have received had he stuck to the business. But then Gaz always had other ideas. A fighter first – he'd already done some training. Then an actor. Or maybe even a singer. Something easy and painless to keep the money and birds ticking over until he really hit the big time. He tolerates Davey's greenhornness, his usurpation of Gaz's barrow boy birthright because Davey listens to him. Unlike most of his crew, Davey admires Gaz for being his own man, for breaking away. And for grudgingly including him in his Lucknow chalk talks.

Davey is full of the fight on last night's television. 'Did you see McCrory? He took that spic apart piece by piece. Did him good and proper.'

'Nah,' says Gaz taking a long sip, 'I was busy.'

Davey's attention crystallizes to a diamond point.

Busy is a great buzz-word with Gaz's crew. Busy is a form of business and business is the only business. Done right (though not necessarily by the book) it pays out, like a bent fruit machine, a regular stream of money and girls. Gaz hasn't offered to buy Davey's drink so Davey knows he hasn't been money-busy; that only leaves sex.

'Yeah, so what you been up to – or *who*?'

Gaz says nothing, just looks intently and importantly out the front door. Calculating.

'You had it off with Queenie, didn't you?'

Gaz splutters into his glass. Queenie is a neighbourhood dosser whose hair is the consistency of congealed spaghetti. At opening every night she settles at the largest table, knowing that as it fills up somebody will feel sorry for her and buy her a drink. (I slip her the odd whiskey now and again. We Untouchables look after our own.)

Davey's put a good one over on Gaz and milks it. 'It was Queenie, wunnit Gazza? Old toothless Queenie,' and he starts to laugh.

'Aw leave it out, Davey. Fuckin' hell, no need to wet yourself.' Nobody else has entered the pub and Gaz is getting angry. He's got to tell somebody and Davey's just blown his chance, braying there like an ass. What Gaz really needs are mates more his own age – geezers a bit more mature, a bit more sophisticated. Geezers who will appreciate the intricacies and raptures of the chase and capture. He drains his glass, goes to the door. Not a soul in sight. Jack Jones again.

Davey's still giggling. 'You want another drink, Gaz?' He dumps a wad of notes onto the counter. Gaz looks hard at the money then at Davey. It's mostly twenties with the odd fifty poking through.

'Good day on the stall yesterday,' Davey smiles. 'Busy.' His heavy gold bracelet, bought last night in the Boswell's Head, glints.

For a second Gaz is defeated, utterly lost. Then just as utterly he has a brainstorm.

'Pint of lager-top mate.'

I am brought to a halt by his next conversation – not by the content but the recipient.

Me.

The bar extension. The dregs.

'Who'd you think's the best-looking bird comes in here?'

'Ah – '

'Come on, you're the bartender. You serve 'em all. You're not blind. You gotta have an idea.'

I recover gradually and fish for a half-knowing smile. 'I . . . um . . . take the Fifth.'

'Which fifth?' puzzles Davey, scanning the back bar. This is a new game and he doesn't know the rules.

Gaz slips me a wink. I find myself winking back. Complicity makes for strange caste systems.

'*The* Fifth,' he explains pedantically. 'One of them American legal terms. Like on *The Streets of San Francisco*. Means he ain't sayin'.'

'Oh.' The tables have been turned on a dime; Gaz presses on.

'So who'd'you think?'

I know the correct answer and lay it before him, hyping it with just the right touch of awe: 'Michelle.'

'And who was in here last night, all night?'

'Michelle.'

'Was she in here alone?'

'Why no, I don't believe she was.' (I fight down a tendency to ham my responses.) Davey's eyes are glued to Gaz, whose tone shifts from brisk QC to casual man of the world, posing a question whose answer is a foregone conclusion. 'Who did she leave with?'

'Why you of course, Gazza.'

My reply touches off two divergent repercussions: Davey looks like he's been cracked over the head with a pint jug and Gaz, who's never heard his name on my lips let alone in its familiar form, gives me a warning glare. Witness is excused. I turn my attention to Davey's pint, which he's knocked over.

In a world where men age bloatedly and women overnight Michelle was fresh and free as falling water. A glow of youth shone all through her – her beauty swept like a beacon over Dickens Estate, occasionally exposing a balding beergut knocking off a rouged-over wrinkle, and passing on. Her own mother was such a wrinkle, a middle-aged housewife dawdling on the dole; her father an Italian seaman, current whereabouts unknown, presumed knocking someone off back in Italy.

Michelle – named French by her mother to spite her father – came into the Lucknow often, always in the protection of a gaggle of girls who sat in one corner sipping Malibu and pineapple and eyed their out-of-pub boyfriends, who sat in the other and took no notice. Why Michelle came along I have no idea, except perhaps she was checking the fit of off-the-peg Dickens Estate existence prior to moving up to *haute couture*. She possessed no out-of-pub boyfriend – had endless aspirants both sides of the Lucknow door but never took them up – and on the night of the seeing-to the rumor was that the very next day she'd be lost for ever, swallowed up by the incomprehensibly Geordie world of Leeds University.

To Gaz's crew she was the ultimate pull. When her round came up all other activity would halt and a churchlike silence descend as she passed among them. Once at the bar, though, it was every man for himself: offer her a smoke or a match or a line of chat or, if they'd been busy, buy her round. She always declined smiling. They never pushed it the way they did with other girls. She would sashay back to her table with an armload of Malibu and pineapple, silence descending once again, broken here and there by half-spoken mutterings as each man invoked curse or blessing on her soul. That the only person on Dickens Estate earmarked for transcending it was both a girl and a darkie was something they could never come to terms with. Gaz especially, because in his mind that earmark was meant for him.

I've finished mopping up Davey's drink and, having performed my interlocutor's duties, now stand with my back to the bar, drying glasses and surreptitiously consulting the back bar mirror. Gaz is winding up his account of last night's events. It differs from my memory only in the heroic quality Gaz attributes to himself – the epic myth is alive and well and being sung not by bards but barrow boys. Davey is enraptured, although his face clouds over when Gaz skips through the post-pub agenda with Michelle with almost no regard for detail. Did she get a right old seeing-to or not? Gaz seems to think so. Davey lets it go because the rest of the story is so good. Gaz finishes with the image of himself rampant against the rosy-fingered dawn, virgin-voided bedsheet of victory snapping behind him. Davey is agog with the glory of manhood.

'Fuckin' hell Gazza,' he whispers, 'fuckin', fuckin' hell.'

The next day at precisely eleven-fifteen I set a lager-top fizzing on the bar. By eleven-thirty it has gone flat. Davey's brother Terry comes in at twenty to twelve, Davey a few seconds later. Both make straight for the lager-top. Both look agitated. Terry waves off my query of a drink. He points to the pint.

'He been in yet?'

I shake my head.

'Bastard.'

'What you want him for?' says Davey.

'Connaughton,' snaps his brother, 'Manor House middle-weight. Gaz was supposed to go a few rounds with him last night.'

'I didn't hear nothin' about that.'

'Yeah, well you're a kid, i'n't ya?' Davey looks hurt. Terry acquiesces. 'We had to keep it quiet. There was a couple quid involved. Didn't want the Old Bill fishing round in our pockets.'

Davey nods seriously. 'So what happened?'

'Gaz didn't show's what happened. Lost his bottle. I thought maybe he was with that Michelle bird – ' A possible leer of admiration traces Terry's mouth. ' – You know, that Itie bint everyone's saying he – '

Now it's Davey's turn to be in the know. 'Bollocks!' he explodes. 'She's in fuckin' Leeds. Besides, he never knocked her off anyway. *She* knocked *him* off.' He snorts derisively. 'More like blew him off.'

'What?' says Terry. This is news. I creep a little closer myself.

'I was talking to her sister on the stall and she says it was *Michelle* done *Gaz*. Gave him a right old seeing-to. Said Michelle had some fuckin' crazy idea – she wanted to – you know – sort of have it away like proper before she went to university. Or some such women's libber shit like that.'

'Michelle? A *libber*?' Practically a dyke.

'Yeah – makes you wonder, dunnit? But listen – her sister says she picks Gaz, right, because he's *harmless*. You know, sort of stupid. So she let him chat her up that night, right, and buy a load of drinks, just so's she could get a bit of libber's wham-bam-thank-you-Gaz.'

Terry is speechless.

'So they gets back to his place, he locks his mum out an' they start going at it like the clappers. On the settee.' Davey sniggers. 'Only fuckin' Gaz can't get it up.'

'No,' gasps his brother.

'Yes. Like a limp salami's our Gazza. Brewer's droop. Or worse. Half the night Michelle's trying to get him up. And when she does, her sister says he don't know what to do with it.'

'Christ,' moans Terry.

'Where to put it, how to use it – he might've stuffed it up his arse for all the good it was doin' him. So she gave up. Left him there at half-mast and walked out. Laughing like a drain she was, according to her sister. Bumped into his mum in the corridor, which only made her worse. Sister said the sound of her laughing woke her up three flights down.'

Suddenly there is bitterness in his voice. 'The cunt. The stupid cunt.'

After a profound silence Terry chortles, an older brother chortle. He sets Davey straight: 'Just like Gaz. Never could do nothin' right. All mouth and no trousers, that's Gazza. Now if it'd been me locked in there with Michelle . . .' he is stopped by the door slamming. Gaz's mother Peg, nose, ears and eyebrows struggling out of a wallow of wrinkle cream, careers into the pub.

'Where is he?' she spits.

'Don't know – ma'am,' sputters Davey, taken aback by the wildness in her eyes.

'His things are gone. I comes into his room this morning to wake him up so's he can cash his Giro and his wardrobe's empty. An' he's gone.'

Gaz has left without his dole money. This is unheard of. His mother looks from Terry to Davey. Terry shrugs; Davey straightens up on his stool. Peg leans heavily on the bar. She sighs loudly and, possibly, matronly.

'You just can't control them these days. Oi barman – what's yer name – '

'Jim.'

' – Jim. Give me a large gin and tonic. And half a Guinness.'

For a second all three are lost in thought. I take away the lager-top, which jolts them back. 'In a ladies' glass,' snaps Peg. 'And another thing – ' she half snaps, staring at me preparing it, ' – what's that little dago tart doin' sneakin' round my hallway last night?' She takes the drink from me before I can set it down. 'And why is one of my good sheets out on the line, covered in blood? He been fighting again?' She gets no answer from her gin and tonic, and by the time she's into the Guinness her son doesn't exist.

'So that whole story he told me yesterday ain't even true,' mutters Davey. 'Stupid cunt.' He motions for a bitter shandy.

'One thing's for sure,' says Terry, 'he ain't gonna show his fuckin' face round here for a long time. Pint of lager, mate.' I jump to comply.

And I think: if I wanted I could move up a second caste in as many days. For I possess the enlightenment these three boozing Brahmans so tirelessly seek.

I saw Gaz this morning.

It was at King's Cross station. I was coming out of the tube on my way to work. He was in a queue at one of the platforms.

The sign said Leeds. His dress was studiedly casual but his demeanor blew his cover. His Sergio Francini bag drooped from his slumping shoulders. He was swilling from a can of supermarket lager he brought to his stubbly mouth in a frequent cigarette-like attack. He looked bottomed-out. He looked seen-to.

As he tilted his head back to capture the dregs his bag slipped off his shoulder, taking most of his fashionably baggy Georgio Avanti shirt with it. Along his collarbone a long snakelike gash of plaster emerged. He regarded it almost wistfully, then shrugged his shirt back on.

He remained in the queue until he reached the barrier, at which point there was some kind of problem. The ticket-taker pointed repeatedly to the ticket booth on the concourse, finally turning Gaz around and giving him a gruff push in its direction. He faltered after a few steps, paused, took everything around him in slowly, like a closing shot in a film, before finally shuffling out among the bums on Pentonville Road, his empty can cleaved to his bosom like a lost love.

So his secret's safe with me. I make his mother another gin and tonic. The whole world could be searching for Gaz and I wouldn't let on, not for all the tea in China. Not for all the chilli dogs in New Jersey. Not for all the *bhajis* in Bombay.

It's caste loyalty really. We Untouchables look after our own.

Nutrasweet

On the morning of her forty-first birthday, the day she couldn't imagine living past, Connie Bettencourt slipped on a sourball wrapper. There was nobody else in her apartment; the bottom half of her building was a bankrupt feed store, and there was nobody there either. So she fell alone, forty-one and friendless, her only solace the bookcase straining, stretching, yearning to comfort her aching temple with a reassuring buttress of solid oak –

Her sliding foot kicked out her other and changed her direction.

And a few moments later Connie was on her way back to work.

'How ya doin' there, Connie,' said Ward as she nosed her second-hand Opel up to the barricade at the Rolling Hills guard-house, 'how's effrythin'?' His A-1 security badge, modeled, he boasted, on the one at the end of *Dragnet*, bristled on his modified bellhop's suit.

'Fine and dandy, Ward.'

'You have a good birthday party last night? You're lookin' pretty chirpy.'

'Well you know . . . after forty, all water off a duck's back.'

Ward didn't know. He was twenty-two. 'Well all I know's, after all that wine there you were floatin' like a duck while the rest of us're sinkin' like stones.'

Connie looked anxiously towards the sales office. She had left home in a daze and forgotten her breakfast cigarette. Nicotine, her brain screeched.

'Stamina, I guess. Comes with years of abuse.'

'Guess so.' He pushed the button to raise the barricade.

Connie heard the simulated pine door of the sales office swish shut behind her. Her Dr Scholl's sank into the institutional-plush carpet like a kidnap victim into chloroform. Her first order of the day, as every day, was to dump the contents of her battered pocketbook onto the painted-pine reception desk and hunt for her cigarettes. That accomplished, she embarked upon the fouling of several feet of fresh Hunterdon County air with greying belches of smoke, which she gently waved to the corners of the room. Finally she opened the maw of her pocketbook at the edge of the desk and commenced dragging everything back in.

Today it took several attempts. Scraping and clattering sounds jumped in the air. Connie smiled. On the surface this was a day like any other – the morning ritual of smoke and sound staving off the hoodoo of a soulless workspace. She wondered how much longer she'd be able to keep this up – how long before she died. She scuffed across the carpet to her office and a wheezy conference with her ashtray.

A few minutes later Jean Anne came by. Jean Anne lived in a Danforth town house, an ex-sales model, at the far end of Rolling Hills. She was in the habit of always checking the other sales models on her way to work.

'Mornin' Miz Bettencourt?' she called apprehensively.

'Morning Jean Anne. In here. What's the damage today?'

Connie liked Jean Anne. She came from a failed farm too near the megalomaniac Route 80, a big strapping girl struggling with a world she believed saw her only in terms of mud-wrestling or the Olympic shot-put. But still she was trying. She had ploughed through all the Succeeding In Business And Life bestsellers and was even now engaged in Controlling Emotion. She was new to it – seeing Connie caused her to collapse against the doorway, a look of screaming relief swamping her face.

'Oh-thank-God-you're – um, somebody's swiped one of the vases in Thorneycroft. And – and somebody's written "fuck you" across the breakfast note in the Peacehaven master bedroom.'

'Bully for them. What a shame Mr Della Salla can't see it.' Connie would have sent the note to Della Salla, had she known where he was. He'd come up with the idea – a handwritten note next to the plastic bacon and eggs on the breakfast tray saying, 'Good Morning! Welcome to Peacehaven! We know you'll agree breakfast tastes better in your custom-built Rolling Hills dream home!! Love, Dynamicorp.' He'd come up with a lot of ideas. One of them, a 1,000-dollar deposit left with him to ensure nobody else got your custom-built dream home first, had led to his untimely departure. And Connie's elevation from Rolling Hills receptionist almost a year ago.

(Connie had liked Della Salla too, in a way – to be dishonest requires imagination, and lately she had run out of that. An asthmatic childhood, a philandering father, a mother institutionalized like clockwork every time he didn't come home, two failed marriages, twenty solid years of temporary jobs leading to too many cigarettes leading to chronic bronchitis . . .

'Well, yez know what they sez,' Della Salla had grinned, 'when life gives yez lemons, yez makes lemonade.'

'I've tried, for forty years so far. It's sour.'

Della Salla had leaned far, too far over the reception desk. 'Nutrasweet, baby, nutrasweet. Little man-made sugar. Yez can't wait for Muthuh Nachuh come sweeten things up for yez. Gotta do it yezelf.' His breath smelled like old socks.

Three days later he had vanished.)

'I'll write out another note,' announced Jean Anne, 'and I'll drive over to Phantasmagoria at the mall and get another vase.'

'God, no, not Phantasmagoria. Phantasmagoria's even tackier than we are. Peacehaven looks enough like a battlefield without Phantasmagoria.'

'Huh.' With its Toulouse-Lautrec prints and repro stripped-pine suites Jean Anne thought Phantasmagoria quite stylish.

Connie had a sudden flash of inspiration. 'Listen, have we still got those empty wine bottles from last night?'

'What, the faggy ones with the paintings on the labels?'

'Yes, the faggy ones with the paintings on the labels.'

'Yeah. Somewhere.'

'Good.' Connie went to a cabinet at the back of the office, flinging the doors open with a gesture that was pure props mistress. A moment later she returned with a single red plastic rose and two wine glasses. 'Here. Stick this on the table in one of those faggy wine bottles. And set these glasses around it. But don't just plop them down, give it some life, OK?'

'Life – OK,' managed Jean Anne. She was Controlling Emotion again. She walked stiffly out of the room.

Connie went back to work. She suddenly realized she was humming. That silly little stupid idea just now was responsible. Nutrasweet, baby, nutrasweet – but while she hummed it was the idea of death which seemed silly. She hummed some more.

'Um, Miz Bettencourt,' Jean Anne was at the doorway again.

Connie looked up.

'I, ah, just wanna say, um, in light of what you like told me last night – '

Connie's hum hiccupped in her throat.

' – Well just thanks for being here today . . . I mean, when I like walked in that door this morning I – Alive,' and she fled the office, uncontrolled.

Another in a seemingly endless string of bad decisions, Connie thought, an oil slick spreading through the turbid sea of her life. Last night. She grabbed for a cigarette, lit it, suffered a long bronchial cough.

Last night had been her forty-first birthday party. Jean Anne had organized it a day early so that at midnight she could be first to say Happy Birthday. Connie, deciding that any sendoff was better than no sendoff at all, had played along, even to the extent of sweet-talking the bartender at the Rolling Hills social club into donating a couple of bottles of wine Dynamicorp usually gladhanded around to new home owners. Her droopy eyelashes had fluttered appreciatively; he'd been almost as stunned as she by her twenty-year-old show of coquetry.

Ward had shown up, badge gleaming, along with a squadron of security guards. Jean Anne had invited a few girls from her Distributive Education class, and everyone had driven out to one of the new unfurnished Peacehavens at Walden – a tract of high, isolated land with a view of the Delaware Water Gap so rare Connie found it unnerving.

Perhaps it was that, perhaps the Dynamicorp wine caroming around Connie's empty stomach, perhaps Ward's noseguard blocking of Jean Anne's raw-boned advances, which isolated Connie and Jean Anne at the night's close. They finished perched side by side in the uncompleted fireplace, a bottle of wine between them, watching flames licking at Ward and Alicia. Jean Anne cried, declaimed about the unfairness of her life, and cried some more. Connie held out a pack of Kleenex usually reserved for bronchitis attacks. Jean Anne dabbed at her eyes and asked sniffingly how this birthday party was measuring up to all the others.

Connie, who'd spent a lot of time staring out at that rare view and the steep drop-off which made it possible, couldn't remember. Not one birthday party, never, not all her life. All there was was exhaustion, dogging equally forty birthdays and forty in-betweens – those moments by the screeching telephone, one twitchy hand poised, trying to beat back bad news in advance . . .

'Well, considering I'm not going to live past forty my forty-first's going pretty good.'

Words dropped like red wine into the carpet.

Connie winced. Yet how else to explain to a teenager keening for a crack at life that yours has been more than you requested and you haven't been very impressed and frankly don't know where to summon the energy for any more? Not that you're desperate for death, just that you, at this particular stocktaking, seem to have run out of life the way most people do groceries? Forty was going to be it, the end, *finito*. Connie's manager's mind had long ago put two neat black lines through forty-one et seq., assuming they would be cancelled due to lack of interest. Yet here she was turning to that page, the Walden bluff offering a last-ditch opportunity to square accounts.

Jean Anne stared slackjawed at Connie for a moment, during which the rest of the world just slipped away. It returned slowly but resolutely; Jean Anne looked at Connie hard, measuring. Connie felt another duplicitous hum of pleasure as someone lardered with life, someone still chipping away at it, broke through a little, suddenly understood a small corner of its complexity.

Then Jean Anne burst again into tears. 'Oh, that's *sad*,' she wailed, 'that's just *so sad*.'

Connie had stayed with her the rest of the evening.

There was a mark – Della Salla's word – in the office when Connie returned from lunch. She was glad, and not. Lunch in her favorite diner, supposedly a cure for the hangover of last night's memories, had been consumed in solitude and mounting confusion, interspersed with mental picture postcards of the Walden bluff. What she needed was a little afternoon constitutional out that way – what she needed was the only worthwhile attribute of this job: professional abnegation. Complete immersion in a stranger's life. The selflessness of the successful saleswoman. Ah, thought Connie, seductive success. By now a very moldy carrot on the end of a brittle, crooked stick, but it still attracts.

Jean Anne was nowhere to be seen. Connie stole one last glimpse out the window, then made a show of hurrying out to the man. 'I'm terribly sorry. Our receptionist must still be at lunch. Have you been waiting long, Mr . . .?'

'Wilson.' He was tall, angled, with two tufts of white hair sprouting like seedy cat-tails above each ear.

'I'm Connie Bettencourt, Mr Wilson. Sales Manager. And I am very sorry about your wait.'

He waved it off. 'Well, now you're here let's go have a look-see. I'm mighty curious 'bout what you've all done here.'

He certainly wasn't giving much away. Usually by now Connie would have cataloged the mark as either window shopping or serious. However: no ring on finger, possible no wife so no grandchildren factor – probably one of the Abercrombies overlooking the water sports area, small yet cheerful, low maintenance charge, close to the Cumberland Farms and nondenominational chapel, very popular with Golden Agers we find – Connie smiled her professional smile. He looked nervous, then returned the smile. Warmly. All things considered, she was a great immerser. Professionally, a success.

They went in his car, a new blue compact with Florida plates. He drove it like a farm tractor, sitting bolt upright, scouting for bumps and ditches and yanking the car around them at the last possible second, posting smoothly through the lurches. She fed him the usual Rolling Hills pitch – location, amenities, land value, serenity – accompanied by lots of smiling, eye contact and repetition of his name. She hardly noticed the bumps.

He seemed to know where he wanted to go – within a few minutes the car had swung onto the Walden Road.

And like a remand prisoner being flung back inside, like a psychic forced to board the doomed flight, Connie found herself back at Peacehaven. Wilson killed the motor. At the bottom of the bluff a pheasant shrieked.

'You've been to Rolling Hills before?' Her voice came to her as if from off the bluff: edgy, unprofessional.

'You could say that.' Wilson got out of the car and opened the trunk. He was humming. As Connie watched he shouldered a clanking burlap bag. He struck out for the bluff.

It was like something out of an old B movie. And Connie had lived through enough real-life B movie slots to recognize B movie suspense. It annoyed her that so near the climax of her own she was still a contract player – even now there was so much being directed by others. Inflamed, and surprised by it, she stamped after him.

She found Wilson at the far corner of the Peacehaven lawn underneath a monolithic oak tree. He was ripping up the grass. He looked up, a neat square of sod balanced in his knotted, sawtooth-edged fingers.

'Ya know,' he said, 'a good manager would be on her walkie-talkie by now, screamin' like hell at those boy scouts there at the front to wake up 'n' save her from the crackpot out at Squaw's Leap.'

Connie hadn't brought her walkie-talkie with her. 'Walden,' she said after a bit, 'it's called Walden. After the Thoreau Walden.'

'It's called Squaw's Leap. Used to whitewash the rock where she did it every spring, till I got tired of pickin' all the botched suicides off the bluff. Jilted lovers a lot of 'em, just like her. Painted it brown after that. Never got bothered again.' He shook his head.

Connie laughed, unexpectedly. It felt arthritic. 'I know who you are,' she said after another bit. 'You're *the* Wilson. Wilson of the Wilson Tract. The farmer who made a killing selling all this land to Dynamicorp ten years ago. The one they named the road the office is on after. You're *that* Wilson.'

Wilson chuckled, a wheeler-dealer's chuckle. 'Yep, I'm *that* Wilson. And *this*,' he pointed to the pared lawn, 'is my house.' He tapped it with his foot. 'Drove all the way up from Florida to get my hands on it.' From his bag he drew a collapsible spade. Connie watched him turning the earth in smooth, even strokes. It came up brown and loamy, the color of his hands.

After a few minutes digging he looked up. 'So you're not gonna go and sic them pretend police on old Bryden Wilson, are ya?'

Connie felt her head shaking no. To hell with pretend police. To hell with Dynamicorp. Something was happening here and she didn't know what it was – a song she hadn't thought of for years. Her first husband, just out of high school, used to play it nonstop on a guitar she'd got selling Christmas cards door to door. And his name was Jones. Mr Jones.

'Didn't think so.' Wilson grunted. 'Some manager.'

'What are you digging for?'

'You'll see.' He leaned on his spade. A fieldstone foundation was emerging. 'My family built this,' he clanked the spade against it, 'so many great-greats back I can't remember. Legend has it one of 'em's buried under that cedar over there.' He pointed at a lone tree overhanging Squaw's Leap. Connie followed and noticed most of the branches on the cliff side had been lopped off. 'Had to do that too. Like they say about giving folks enough rope. Round here everything from the Depression to that new superhighway there gave 'em plenty. Me, I was lucky. I bought out. Right around the time I started gettin' old and farmin' started turnin' into ag-ree-business. Right around the time my sister Sissie died.' He was shoveling again, his spade churning a steady cadence, his speech matching it like a hammer to a railroad spike. 'We farmed here, just us two, thirty-two years like man and wife. Did all right – nights on the porch drinkin' cold sun tea, lookin' out at the view. Thinkin' all the time, it don't come better than this.' Wilson was now in a sizable trench, which he motioned Connie to help him out of. 'And it didn't. Thanks. She's out here too ya know. She loved the woods, much more 'n me. I'm a field man. She loved nothin' better 'n a wander, an afternoon mosey through these trees, bringin' me my lunch pail out in my fields.' His eye winked like sun through trees. 'Many's the time I didn't eat till close to quittin'. She made me promise to plant a beech over her when she went, on account of they grow real fast and that's what she wanted. To be taken up through the roots right up there into the trunk, out on the tip of a twig that first warm day of Spring – yessir.' He wiped his misty face with a handkerchief.

Connie was wondering, what was the name of that song? She watched Wilson hitch up his pants, hop back into the trench, resume digging.

'Couldn't take my house with me when I sold up either. Two hunnert years old, summer beam size of a man's hand, all in a mall over Flemington way now. Whole place loaded on the back of a flatbed truck. Doin' time as one of them artsy-craftsy places sellin' imitation colonial stuff colonial people woulda laughed halfway to Harrisburg.'

This was incredible – she'd loved that song, the way Jones had played it, all confused and mournful. Then for twenty years she'd utterly forgotten it. Go with it, she felt something tell her, get it. Seek sweetness.

'Have you ever gone to see it?' she asked him.

The dirt flew. 'Yeah. Saw it yesterday. They raised the ceiling. Took the summer beam out. Said customers kept bumpin' their heads on it 'n' complainin'.' He squinted up at Connie. 'Said one of 'em even had to go to the hospital. Concussion.' Wilson leaned back and laughed. It was a rumbling grunt of a sound, the kind bears make scratching their backs against trees.

'Concussion,' he rumbled again. Dirt spewed into the air.

And Connie felt herself laughing too, till her cheek muscles ached. She lit a cigarette. Her body had forgotten about cigarettes. 'Mr Wilson,' she leaned over the pit, 'why did you leave Florida? What are you after?'

'Hate the sun if things 'ren't growing under it. Where I live, the condo Dynamicorp bought me outside Orlando, nothin' grows. Everything bakes. No trees. They flew in topsoil but the first tropical storm washed it away. No ground. No shade. Just busloads of old folks – what do you people call 'em, Golden Agers – all come down to die in the dust. So what do they do? I'll tell ya. Play cards, watch the pulpit-pounders on TV, and argue about whose family's gonna come visit first. And nobody's ever does. So one day I just thought, hell, that's it, I can't stand it any more, I'm gonna zip home for a little visit. So I turn the air conditioner up full blast, whack on the TV and the VCR, plug in the microwave, the food processor, the vacuum cleaner, switch on all the lights – hell, I even turned on my electric toothbrush.' He paused. 'To hi. And off I went.' His wheeler-dealer's smile again. 'Dynamicorp pays all my bills.'

Connie's guffaw exploded in cigarette smoke.

And for the second time in two days she was aware of her eyelashes fluttering.

'An' ya know somethin' Missez Manager,' said Wilson examining a splintered shard of foundation, 'it's good to get out.' He handed it up for Connie's inspection. 'Good to know you can get out.' She rolled it around her palm. It was surprisingly warm. 'Good to find you've still got some life, in front of you as well as behind.' He was watching her, not interferingly but with interest. Like something was happening. She noticed and hurriedly dumped the shard into his upturned hand. He scooped a hole out of the side of the trench, interred the shard, and returned to digging, the corners of his mouth an upturned evanescence.

A few minutes later his spade emitted a high rasping noise. Connie fought back the urge to jump into the hole with him.

'What have you hit? China?'

Wilson didn't answer, instead burrowed woodchuck-like into the ground. There were some frantic shifting sounds, a cry, then he popped up with an old verdigrised milk box under his arm.

'That's what you were looking for, isn't it?'

'You bet.' He heaved it onto the ground at her feet. 'Sissie and I buried it Arbor Day 1932. Sissie'd just been in town for a cornerstone-dedicating ceremony. When the W.P.A.'d just finished that new train station.'

Connie knew the one. It now sold fudge and bric-a-brac.

'So she came home all full of cornerstones – why didn't we have one, and a ceremony, make a list of what to put in it, and suchlike. So we did. On Arbor Day, to make it easy to remember. And we planted that – ' he pointed to the tree overshadowing the lawn – 'red oak, New Jersey state tree, as a reminder above ground of our reminders below.' He contemplated the box the way Connie imagined him contemplating the view all those years ago. 'A fine day.'

'Well,' she finally ventured, 'well, what's in it?'

He scratched his head. 'Can't say as I remember. And that's been buggin' me like thunder for the last fifty years.'

'Well, go on then, open it. Open it.' She had to say that quickly because her bronchitis was swarming. Her laughter had brought it on. She scrabbled in her pocketbook for her Kleenex, remembering too late she'd given them all to Jean Anne.

She managed to half-turn away as the attack began. It was long, loud and vituperative, swearing vengeance. She could feel herself crying as she struggled to bring up the mucus flooding her throat. She was erupting in gagging fits, frenzied for breath.

Wilson looked up startled.

When the attack had finally subsided Connie's first thought was, as always, of Kleenex. Her second was of Jean Anne; her third, triggered by the rare feel of comforting arms squeezing her shoulder and softly rubbing her back, was an inner cry of confusion – not one, never, not all my life. Her fourth was of Della Salla, somewhere glutting man-made lemonade.

Her fifth, the Walden bluff, was interrupted by Wilson's rumble: 'You OK?' She nodded weakly. 'Bronchitis?' She nodded again. He gently released her to the cushion of piled sod. 'Sissie had it as a kid. You oughta look after yourself better.' She nodded again, her eyes averted. She was looking at his shoes. Muddy brown wingtips – he dug ditches in his Sunday shoes. Her father once had a pair the same color in the same shape. He sometimes let her clomp around the entranceway in them. They made a delightful racket, it was the middle of blooming, squelching spring and of course mud would fly everywhere.

When the color had returned to her cheeks he asked her if the Pittstown Inn still did those terrific double-decker hot roast beef sandwiches.

Her tangled hair jerked yes.

He picked up his box. It rattled.

'Well, we need some kinda ceremony, don't we?'

Connie looked up. She could barely breathe, her head was hammering, her eyes and mouth had gushed liquid down her blouse, her eyes were bugged out puffy and raw. Her heart was beating a desperate tattoo against her ribcage. She felt like death.

Wilson rattled the box again.

Her cheek muscles ached. 'We do.'

Vive La Perspective(s)!

HE stood in the middle of the village square, which to his trained artist's eye couldn't really be called either. A village had some semblance of activity, of human inter- action, somewhere between, say, Constable and Hogarth, and a square consisted of four sides. This one only had two. The others had been blown down ages ago by the same ceaseless wind which roared around him, through him. Buffeting his very soul. This place was the edge of the world.

He was leaning against an ancient rusted petrol pump, waiting for Ticia, who was supposed to be taking the shot, to tell him hold it right there he looked so windswept he was overpowering the landscape. When she didn't and Justin grew tired of the stinging smack of his long convoluted cowlick against the bridge of his nose he brought his hand up, moodily, and tossed the hair out of his face. This revealed Ticia, her back to him, her hair swept up off the gleam of her neck and roiling about her ear. He frowned.

Ticia was over by the land's end, hands jammed in pockets, staring at the gulls and skuas lounging miles up in the offshore thermals. Justin sighed. He abandoned his pose and slouched over to her.

'Look at them,' she said, 'the perfect expression of freedom. Ah, if only I could paint, paint like you *chéri* I'd paint them. Up there. There in all their emancipated glory. Capture that – that rapture of movement, that delicate *pas de deux* with the sky.' She sighed.

Justin shifted impatiently. 'Well, that's my *métier*. You're the one who's the photographer, remember?'

'Yes of course,' she said, eyes still heavenward.

'Well, *faits attention! Regarde!*' He snapped his fingers in front of her. *Regarde, chérie!*' He turned her inland. 'The textures, the space, the interplay of light and shadow, the way the wind gnarls and grotesques the landscape . . . I thought that's why we agreed to take that detour and come out here. I thought we agreed the solitude, the starkness would better expose our feelings. Stimulate our creativities.' He could already see the exhibition program: 'A document in oils and photography of transcendent love affirming and solidifying its timeless commitment amidst the disillusion and dissolution of post-nuclear *anomie*.' He could write too. He swept his hand through his hair again. 'I can't do it alone, you know.'

'This place does look like a bomb hit it,' said Ticia.

'Just like I told you, *chérie*. Which is why it's perfect.' Justin softened; seeing Ticia's exposed neck brought out those affirming and solidifying feelings which had inspired him in the first place. His arms slipped through hers, his thumbs hooking into the waist of her faded jeans. His lips tickled at the downy hair around her collar. 'And so are we. And I've got this perfect idea for a perfect *noir* shot of me against this perfect petrol pump . . .' He gently bumped the backs of her knees with his. He steered her firmly towards the square, his hands before her, framing the scene.

At dinner the lovers held hands over the candlelit table and ordered a grilled fish dish, a regional speciality they had previously tasted inland during their tour. 'The difference here is,' Justin leaned forward, seeing the light throwing juddering expressionistic shadows on the cracked wall and working himself in, 'the fish is all pulled fresh from the sea, probably by the same weatherbeaten old peasants we saw fishing from the cliffs . . . Now that's the way to live, *chérie*,' he artfully withdrew and leaned back in his chair, 'all natural. Fresh fish, fresh fruit and vegetables, lots of salad. Lemon juice and olive oil. A simple home – one of those shepherd's huts we saw dug into a terraced hillside. That would do. That's all I need. Really. And just paint everything around me – the fish, the vegetables. The lemons. Lemons like you've never seen, so full and round and perfect your cheeks would pucker just looking at them. Lemons so real Chardin would – ' Here the meal arrived. The main course looked baldly like frozen fish sticks.

Justin offered no comment, only a cold beady-eyed glare at his plate.

Ticia never discovered what Chardin would have done.

After dinner they went for a walk along the cliffs. Justin had refused the rest of the meal, including a roughly-hewn bowl of ripe figs over which Chardin would have been rapturous. He had then suggested the walk, as a means to explore more ideas for the project. He had become so caught up in his *chérie*'s contribution during the day he'd been seriously neglecting his own, he said.

As they walked the panorama fell into stride beside them and Justin could feel his soul swelling, his whole creative being flooding out. The sun was setting just so, the wind blowing urgently, just the way it should – he felt exhilarant, very wise, and very much in control. When he felt this way things always came easier, seemed to convene of their own accord under some sublime directive from him. And without exception they were perfect. *Très parfait.*

There was an abandoned car in their path, a rusted, burnt-out shell teetering on the tip of the edge of the world, its smashed headlights staring blindly towards the dying sun. Justin instinctively placed himself at the best vantage point.

'An automotive Icarus', he mused, feeling the moment spreading from him and engulfing Ticia. This was a land oraculous with mythology and it was speaking; they would do well to listen. He spread his hands over the peeling vinyl sunroof. 'And this his wings, his chariot, his vessel of hope. Ah, can't you just feel it, *chérie*? Look at the sun out there so heavy and close and seductive – bidding us to lean forward and snatch it from the sky.' Justin did as far as he dared. He contemplated the foaming sea. He turned to his love, who looked subdued to the point of beatitude. He shook his head. 'Yet we are all so earthbound, *chérie*. So cheatingly earthbound.' Slowly she nodded her tangle of curls, Athena's wisdom framed by Aphrodite's spume-sprung locks. 'Mere mortals.' He knew this moment, this communion, must be consummated. 'Nothing more.' Offered as a sacrifice. '*Rien*.' Oh, how he felt the very gods thundering approval!

'Give me your camera,' Justin commanded, 'take off your clothes. Quickly, while the light's still good.' Ticia silently demurred. 'This will be the crux of the exhibition,' he panted, yanking his trouser legs over his shoes and socks, ' – a giant photograph the size of a wall, which I emblazon with a brush. It's perfect – you're the black-and-white, the basic reportage, I'm the color, the underlying *esprit sans peur et sans reproche*. Yes,' he grunted as his trouser legs snagged on the fashionable thick heels of his shoes, 'yes, rocketing with color, dizzying with color!' He was finally naked except for shoes and socks. He ran to a dustbin a few yards away, which he upended. Ticia watched goose-pimpled as he danced with the camera then balanced it on the dustbin, set the automatic timer, and ran back. He arranged her restlessly across the front of the car, flinging an arm here, splaying a leg there, frowning, fluffing and tugging till she grimaced. Then, as the sun bled across the knife edge of the horizon, he parted her. There was a whirring as the timer wound down. 'Now think color,' he hissed as he felt Olympus descending, 'feel color! Become color!'

He still had his shoes and socks on.

THEY continued that night in the dreary hotel bed, their lovemaking riotously inspired. Outside the envious wind drove a few scraggly branches against the window – scratch, scratch, screeatch at the pane like clawing through a crowd to get a good gape at an accident. Justin and Ticia might have noticed, might have thought about stopping and reaching for the shade . . . but they liked the stipple of moonlight on their bronzed skins. They shifted a bit to let it get more of a look-in.

It was probably the lovers' mocking fluidity – a spring and neap, a confluence women's magazines tell us doesn't happen until much later in life and men's magazines don't tell us about at all – which had driven the wind to such distraction. When Ticia scissored her long legs around Justin's and brought him into her it was as though she were behind him as well, gently stirring him, buoying him along. When there was contact she slowly opened her mouth into a wide, wide O as if to accommodate him there as well. Justin's thrusts, long and deep and solid, sent her into the shuddery mattress the same distance each time, not with the brute force of a policeman collaring a thug, but with the confidence of a proud father tossing his laughing daughter in the air. When he came Ticia was halfway through her second and curled herself in a ball around him; he drove, she drove; he gave, she received; she gave, he received. Fifty-fifty split right down the middle, no winners or losers. And after it was over, as he traced for the umpteenth time the sleek curve of her breast with his finger and she smiled at the touch of still-twitching muscle along his hard inner thigh, both basked in a sated special glow. As the wind carried on its raking voyeurism they started again, in front of the window standing up.

IT was swaying in the air, a glistening pendulum ticking off the last reflexive seconds of life. The higher it rose the harder it gasped, the faster the pendulum swung. By the time it had entered the first cloud bank the scales had dulled and movement was detectable only in the pink pulsing of the gills.

It hung like a petrified trapeze artist as the sea, its whilom safety net, receded into fog.

Far above it on the cliff tops, crouched head in hand like gargoyles, were the fishermen. Some dangled feet over the edge, the wind swirling and eddying around them. Others sat back in rude folding chairs staring out at the dawn, watching its cracked and groggy clawing up the cliffs. One or two tossed half-smoked cigarettes, which gleamed and spluttered like damp fireworks as they encountered the day. At one point there was some yelling, and a dark-haired young woman's face inched over the edge. She looked into the abyss. Then there was more yelling and the fish jerked rapidly and harshly upwards.

As it emerged from the fog into a distant line-up of several rough faces and one smooth one, the fish was discovered by the wind. At first the wind only toyed cat- or kite-like with it, causing more shouting above and a redoubling of reeling. Thus encouraged, the wind took the fish and worried it repeatedly against the cliffs, mashing its life into guano-stained crags.

The gulls gathered and began to peck.

When the fish was finally winched free under the woman's splayed-arms direction it was dead. It landed at Ticia's feet a bloody and gouged-out lump more bait than prize.

SHE looked down with a woman's horror and an artist's attention. Her mind filled with images – flying, swimming, hanging – and she knew at last what it was which had rendered her sleepless after their lovemaking last night, finally expelling her into the pre-dawn gloom. She also knew again that reckless vertiginous feeling of being at the edge. She had felt it yesterday staring at the gulls; freedom, power; one step could change everything. For good. She looked at the fishermen gathered around – smiling, talking, grim crack-toothed faces wide with congratulations. The one still attached to the fish sought her out: his pointer, his lookout, his stalwart number two.

She turned her back and took the step.

THEY were back at the grizened petrol pump, reshooting the *noir* photo from the day before. Ticia was waiting for Justin to compose himself, to get his damn hair out of his eyes. She had been trying hard to see the last few hours from his point of view but this was being hampered by a wild itching to get on with things she hadn't felt since before she met him. Right now his face was just the perfect tint of glassy ashen, the same exhausted shade dominating the entire *mise-en-scène* here at the edge of the world. But that hair – it was too much. Too much Justin, not enough justified. She managed a small grin through her annoyance. Her quirky sense of humor always came through at precisely the wrong time.

She had charged back to the hotel that morning, burst into the room, interrupted Justin's juggernaut snoring with a cry of, 'Your perspective's all wrong!' When he launched dutifully and dozily into another program excerpt she waved him off. 'You do what you want and I'll do what *I* want.' He woke with a start.

He had watched her suspiciously through breakfast – she was *humming* as she buttered her roll left over from last night's fiasco. When he attempted a cautionary monograph on the creative implications of staleness she chirped, 'Well there's more for those who want it', and snatched his roll away and ate that too. She had eaten more violently than usual, like a starving refugee, like someone who obtained nourishment only through eating. When he asked her where she'd been that morning she replied with uncharacteristic flippancy, 'Oh, just fishing', and wolfed another mouthful.

Justin had felt very unsettled. What was needed, he calculated quickly, was a few minutes together back in bed to reaffirm and resolidify – like last night. A humming only to the music of the spheres. However, his intimations of such, as she watched him dressing after breakfast, were met with nothing save a faint omniscient smile. As if he'd just responded correctly in a psychology experiment.

Her smiles had punctuated the rest of the morning like

machine gun bursts or the rapid-fire click of her camera as she lined her beloved up against the edge of the world. 'It's *you* I want to focus on, *chéri*,' she told him as she draped him on his back, half in half out of the car, hands stretched to the sun, several large rocks crumbling on his chest. 'You against the environment,' she called down to the rock outcropping where he clung desperately, the wind frolicking at his feet. 'Man against Nature, that's the only real commitment.' He lay gasping in windblown grit, the fishermen grinning gruffly with their rods at attention at their sides, one rough thonged sandal of each solid on his stomach. 'Now hold it. And stop coughing please, *chéri*.'

'You see what I'm trying to do, what I have to do, don't you? It's just what the exhibition needs.' Now Ticia was smiling, pinning back Justin's cowlick, using a tone of voice never before sullied by the world beyond the bedroom. She stepped back to consider the shot. Another smile – Justin winced. Painfully. Did it fit the shot? She surveyed through the camera – in the foreground countless tiny tornados kicked up by the upstaging wind; in the background the collapsed confusion of timber, tiles and topography; in mid-shot the empty, broken pump, the chagrined *misérable* – it did. Perfectly. She looked up from her lens; the wince was fading. She took the moment, and in the manner of all great artists made it work for her. She smiled once more. Wider. Again her lover was a perfect inverse, more suffering and more pathetically uncomprehending. She snapped the picture, tried still another smile. An even better response – so snap and smile, snap and smile, snap and smile until her mouth ached and she ran out of film.

Later, while she was packing, humming, eager to get back home to her darkroom, Justin appeared. In his hands was a sketch pad, unopened.

'How did it go, *chéri*?'

He threw the pad on the floor. 'That's how,' he said.

She looked up. 'I'm sorry to hear that.'

'I think we should split up.'

'Right now?'

'As soon as we get home. I'll move out of the flat – get myself someplace out of town. Someplace quiet. I just can't work with noise – all the traffic at home, that hell-driven wind out there . . . It drowns out the sound of my own mind. It deafens my creativity. I can't stand it. It makes me feel positively Munchian. I want to scream.'

'Oh.' His studio in the flat was much bigger than her darkroom. Her darkroom was just a closet really. 'What will we do then? What about the exhibition?'

He threw his hands in the air. '*Mon Dieu, je ne sais pas. J'ai mal. Je t'aime*. I can't stop seeing you. You are everything to me.' He considered it for a moment. 'How could I paint? How could I eat? How could I live?' His eyes filled with tears.

Ticia watched him briefly then, overcome with pity, put her arms around him. She loved him, had worked him too hard, and now she was sorry.

'Shhh, shhh,' she whispered gently in his ear. His soft sobs fell muffled into her thick hair. 'Shhh. Don't cry *chéri*. We won't break up. *Jamais. Je t'aime aussi. Absolument jamais, mon petit.*' She pulled back slowly and introduced a little joke. Then she could resume packing.

'*Comment faire, chéri? Nous sommes trop bons dans le sack.*'

Justin smiled weakly. Ticia's Franglaised French, picked up one holiday in Vichy, had always rankled him.

Americana

It was a normal kind of day, the day Harry J first saw those two kids, like as two peas in a pod, strolling down Finn Road to his place. Strolling is actually a bad word – they were city kids just moved out to the country, two of that first invasion few years back, and all the green and space had them a little on edge. Like housecats suddenly tossed outdoors, slinking was what they were doing. Sticking close together and right alongside the curb, slinking cautiously up the road. They had one of those portable personal tape player gadgets – first I'd seen round here – complete with two sets of earplugs so they could both hear whatever it was drowning out the much more musical sounds of late spring in Hunterdon County.

I saw them from my back yard where I was tying up tomatos. They stopped in front of Harry J's old service station, in front of the wooden sign Wendell and I'd lettered back when we were all going into business together, which said 'HARRY J'S – HI-CLASS PARTS'. Wendell was my brief, long-ago husband and Harry J his older brother and senior business partner, and before Wendell charged off to get himself dead in Korea we had a few laughs over that sign. We'd sit in Harry J's forecourt drinking a beer maybe and watching it swaying in the breeze or frozen still as a whitetail deer's caught your smell. That hoary old sign fitted Harry J to a T: he had the hi-classiest junkyard in the continental US. Prided himself on it, too. We've all got something gives us a reason to get up in the morning; keeping up a hi-class junkyard the envy of New Jersey and the world was Harry J's.

And it was, too. I got an old white '63 Ford pick-up always dropping or rusting bits off, and I've seen my share of junkyards. Not that I could've picked up any spares at Harry J's. Nossir. You wanted a new door for your body-rotted Toyota Celica or a Pinto gearshift knob replace the one you chucked at the State Trooper gave you the speeding ticket, you went elsewhere friend, maybe one of the truckers' garages on Route 22, you didn't go down Harry J's. Only class trash got put out to his pasture. Cadillacs, Lincolns, top-of-the-line Oldsmobiles and Chryslers, even a few of your spiffy foreign jobs, BMWs and Mercedes and Limey Jags and Triumphs, which suddenly appeared as their New York- or Philadelphia-commuting owners discovered the hard way they couldn't hack the back roads of Hunterdon. There they all were in the field behind his station, lined up straight in rows, the grass between them cut neat and tidy. Like those ads you see where they want to make a car look all smart and outdoorsy so they whack it down right in the middle of a golf course. Like that.

It was heaven on earth for car lovers, closest most of us in Hunterdon ever came to something wasn't a Chevy Nova or a tractor. Men used to bring their families on weekends and have picnics out among the fishtail Caddies and tanklike Lincolns. We'd watch them pull up and Harry'd go unlock the gate. Kids'd scatter like dust beat from a rug. Wives'd tramp after them yelling lists of picnicking do's and don'ts, and the husbands'd stop for a few words. Every now and then somebody'd actually want something – a door handle or a back seat or the like – but mostly they'd just stand there with us maybe having a slug of beer, talking 'bout work or the weather or the Flemington Fair, then they'd wander off to the field and we'd see them a little later, clucking quietly, staring at broken-down bits of lifestyles they'd never lead. Like Wendell's old black De Soto Harry J's offered fortunes for but won't sell. All while their kids roared and squealed and played Indy 500 and their wives called 'cross the field, what in Heaven's name did they do with the bottle opener. And Harry J and me just sat there, sometimes hand in hand just smiling, taking it in like old folks at family reunions.

So let's get back to these two kids. There they were that afternoon slinking round Harry J's. They were casing the joint, checking it out to see what sort of potential it had for serious mayhem. I could just tell. I watched them through my hurricane fence. Canned whiny music came over on the breeze.

They looked around shiftily. I always thought it impossible for kids to look adult things like shifty (probably because I never got the chance to have any, so they're still a bit foreign to me) but these two had it written all over their faces. In small print, though, so you couldn't see until you got up close. By which time they'd gauged your usefulness for their mayhem and already either discarded you or were busy reeling you in.

To them I was a discard, like in a winning gin hand, and they knew I didn't like them either. I had met them a couple times in Clinton where I go to buy a packet of plain M & Ms and the morning paper. Every time I saw them there they were hassling one of the poor counter girls about batteries for that silly tape player thing they were always plugged into. The combination of that book-end way they looked, like a matched set of something at the Flemington Fair white elephant, made me immediately suspicious. But they were good-looking with it, in a teenage unisex sort of way, the way models look these days in the hairdresser's window I go to. She was a xerox of him with vague curvy bits. It was weird. You knew they were different and you knew to keep an eye peeled when they were around. I did anyway.

Harry J was another story.

The two of them rarely gave me more than a 'Morning Mrs Walmsley' in the paper store. And of course being shifty they knew my name and circumstances long before I knew theirs (Darcy and Marcy d'Levis it turned out – their parents were in advertising in New York and had bought a place out Jutland way). And being plugged into that infernal machine made their conversation just loud enough to grate but not loud enough to make you lean over and pull the plug. Their talk was an endless river of carping and complaining – Clinton was such a hick town, nothing to do, bad TV reception, no batteries, why'd their parents ever leave New York – things that if I was their mother I would've made darn sure they kept to themselves. But I wasn't and I'm not, and instead I'd bite my tongue till it blistered and leave, cursing Wendell, who'd promised we'd raise our kids someplace way back in the woods, away from hassle. Just the three then four then five or more of us.

Damn Wendell.

As I watched through my fence they took out their earplugs. This, I was to learn, was a sign of trouble. A sign they'd stopped thinking and were ready to act. The bell jingled as they slunk into Harry J's.

Harry J was at the cash counter trying to do the Word Game in the newspaper. He could never do the crossword (which I can whip off in ink in 'bout half an hour – I didn't drive the Bookmobile ten years for nothing) and could only do the Word Game. Today's word was 'malevolent' – so far Harry J'd only gotten 'male', 'ale' and 'lent', which he was worried was an unallowable proper noun, when he heard the bell.

'Lent,' he muttered without looking up, 'that wha'-da-ya-call-it past tense of lean, or that damn-fool on-the-wagon holiday roun' Easter?' He thought it was me.

'Um,' said the boy Darcy, a bit taken aback. Harry J looked up. I never say 'Um'.

'Ken I hep you?' he said quickly to Darcy. He put the paper away. 'You want the key to the gate?' He didn't see Marcy because she was hiding behind her brother. I've seen them do this several times. Then she pops out. Makes for a memorable entrance.

'Um,' said Darcy again. He was still working on the 'lent' question.

Marcy popped out. Harry J's eyes about fell out of his head. He thought maybe the Clinton Package Store house brand he kept under the counter slow days was kicking in a little early.

'Lend,' she said brightly. ' "Lent" is the past tense of "lend". The past tense of "lean" is "leaned".'

'The past tense of "lean" is "leaned",' echoed her brother.

Harry J was rubbing his eyes, the way babies do when they wake up. Now it was his turn. 'Um,' he said. Only his 'Um' was a lot more highly pitched. Marcy started fingering a counter display of air-freshener trees, those cardboard things smell like pine hang from your rear-view mirror.

Harry J's particular display of air-freshener trees went back to 1953. I know because he took them off my hands back when I was in that line of work. It was right after I got the news about Wendell and I was desperate for some activity. I'd got to the point where I was just sitting in a chair in the middle of my living room, leaning towards the front step 'cause I *knew* he's just about to tread on it. I just *knew*.

I needed to get out.

Harry J I didn't know like his brother, but he let me keep a whole forest of those damn trees at his place. Trouble with Hunterton County then was everybody's car smelled the same – cows, chicken shit, fertilizer and the like – nobody realized a car could smell of anything else. I didn't sell a lot. Finally I chucked in the job but not before Harry J bought up all my stock. I felt like a flunkie Girl Scout whose parents have to buy all her cookies. But I was grateful. For the company more than anything else. He's got one of those pine trees smelling up his Wagoneer, I got one smelling up my Ford – closest we came over the years to anything formal. (When he left – I'll get to that in a minute – I kept what there was. I'll hang on to it. Sooner or later some New York get-rich-quick artist's bound to open one of those trendy imitation hash joints in one of the closed-down gas stations too far from the new highway. I expect he'll be crying out for some Period Decoration, I believe it's called.

In fact I'll keep all the junk from Harry J till then. He'd bust a gut out there in Ohio or wherever if he knew all that stuff he collected, from cars to cardboard trees, got a new name – Americana – and once we put a man on the Moon everything overnight became a museum piece.)

'Oh, Eisenhower to the max,' said Marcy taking off two of the trees and holding them up to her ears. 'Scope, Darce, new-wave earrings.' She giggled. He giggled back.

'New-wave city Marce,' he said. 'Check out his tie.'

Harry J did. It was a shining example of Americana, an old skinny Flying-A tie from the days when garages were called filling stations and attendants wore uniforms the way bankers wear pinstripes. Harry J'd started out as one of those attendants.

'Part with that tie,' said Marcy, shiftily dropping the trees into her bag.

'Ken I hep you?' Harry J said again. His mind was fogging up.

'Scope the jacket,' said Darcy. 'Emmett's name embroidered on it and everything.' He pulled Harry J's mechanic's jacket off an old dusty coat rack. 'Run you fifty, sixty GI Luvmoneys in the Village.'

'Part with the jacket,' said Marcy.

'Economy-size can of STP says emmett's got a matching hat somewhere,' said Darcy, casing the coat rack. He found it and tossed it to his sister. 'Rack it sideways on your head Marce. Do Wheezer in *The Little Rascals*.'

'Oh-wah-don't-know,' mumbled his sister in a *Little Rascals* voice.

'Oh-wah-don't-know,' mumbled her brother back in the same voice. They laughed together precisely and short.

Harry J didn't put up a fight. He's being reeled in.

'Part with the hat,' said Marcy.

'And the jacket,' said Darcy.

'And the tie,' said Marcy.

'Year's subscription to *Spencer Gifts* says emmett's got an E-Z clip-on pocket shield which allows your shirts total freedom from embarrassing ballpoint stains,' said Darcy.

Harry J wasn't sure what he was talking about. 'It's broke,' he said to be on the safe side.

'Part with it,' said Marcy.

'Um,' said Harry J.

'The effect is the coordinated outfit,' said Darcy. 'Scope the whole Flying-A scene man. They'd die at Danceteria.'

'Cemetery city,' said his sister, 'they'd do the Gary Gilmore over it.' Immediately both were wracked head to foot wth spastic fits. It was like they'd touched a live wire, arms, legs all over the place. They stopped at exactly the same moment, stared at each other. Their eyes rolled back in their heads. It was part of the dance.

Harry J didn't know. He was thinking maybe he ought to call the Clinton Rescue Squad or Sheriff Frobisher or the Annandale Mental Hospital mobile unit or maybe even me, but he didn't. Truth was he was completely agog over those kids. Not because of the way they talked, their private language, but because he already had a thing about kids. He never had any of his own either, and it bugged him from time to time. Like Wendell bugged him from time to time.

Plus only time he'd ever seen twins that much alike was a pair of pickled Siamese ones at a sideshow in Cementon, Pa. And those didn't dance.

So he sold Darcy and Marcy the Flying-A jacket, tie, *Little Rascals* hat, even threw in two old Flying-A pocket snow scrapers Marcy said she could plough up her hair with at Danceteria. Harry J thought maybe it was an Automat or something for chorus girls. He'd been to New York twice I think.

He made $6.42 on the deal.

He also treated them to a Coke from his old Coke ice chest ('mega-multi Luvmoneys at Bowery Bill's Memorabilia Shop' reckoned Darcy, and Marcy looked ready to buy it) and generally tried to keep them there long as possible, showing them the junkyard and fussing over them like a long-lost grandfather. They stayed awhile but, like grandchildren, not that long, and when I saw them later plugged back in, slinking down Finn Road with all their Flying-A booty, I was still suspicious, but I figured that was that.

I was wrong. They came back next day. I know because I was there, doing the weekend crossword while Harry J, looking choked in his good Elks tie, was sweeping out the forecourt. From a distance they made me do a double take – walking side by side in thirty-year-old filling station gear they could've been – but they weren't.

Nervy they were. 'Gainful employment city,' said Marcy.

'July we fly,' said Darcy.

'Seasonal Manhattan migration. Hang from the trees of the concrete jungle. Scope?' said Marcy.

Harry J thought he was beginning to. He ummed and ahhed for a minute.

'What ken ya do?' he asked. He was thinking he was casting director in those old Gold-diggers movies, like here came the kids' Big Break.

'Ah wants tuh pump gas, Mistuh Clampett,' said Marcy.

''N' Ah wants tuh polish up them cars, Sher'ff Taylor,' said Darcy. They knew their TV. They giggled slightly.

Harry J said yes immediately. I was flabbergasted. I forgot all about the weekend crossword. Harry J'd never had help in his life! Harry J ran a strictly one-man operation! (At least that's what he told me after the air-freshener trees disaster when I'd asked to work for him.) I jumped up and tried not to run into the forecourt.

Harry J heard me coming. 'Well, I ain't gettin' any younger,' he called. His Elks tie looked ready to strangle him.

They were there a month, after school and weekends from May to June, and didn't do a lick of work when he wasn't around. Bone idle I saw them, Darcy reading comics in the back seat of the De Soto with the door open and his skinny legs sticking out, the rags he was supposed to be washing the car with blowing off 'cross the field. Marcy spent most of her time on Harry J's office phone and you could tell by her wild movements she wasn't talking about what to wear to 4H Club. But soon as Harry J – who'd taken to driving out to real hick places like Doddtown and Walnut Creek and Cook's Crossroads, haunting church bazaars and junk shops and scrapyards – returned they'd be darting round like minnows in a brook, all here, there and everywhere. But twitchily and furtively like they had something to hide.

Which it turns out they did.

One Saturday in early June I saw Harry J's Wagoneer pull out of the forecourt. Now I'd never seen him leave the station on a Saturday ever, so I decided to tail him. By the time I caught up he'd already done his business. A rusted old gas station pump, one of those with the flattened fishbowl tops looks like the man from Mars was stashed in the back of the Wagoneer.

'It's amazin' Hattie,' he told me in the tavern I'd dragged him into to explain, 'what kids these days don't know. What with all their battery-operated gizmos percolatin' noise, they don't know nothin' 'bout the past. Those two keep seein' pitchers like in the old magazines, and stuff hangin' round the station, en they say "scope" this and "part with" that. They got no sense of Merkan history. So if I gets a minute I zips out en finds 'em some.'

I shook my head slowly.

'I feel it's my duty,' he said, 'as an Merkan and an Elk.'

He was really starting to go.

So it came as no surprise that night in late June. It was cold and I had the windows closed else I would've heard much sooner. As it was, by about two a.m. the ruckus from the field was so loud my windows were rattling in their sashes. I threw on some clothes and ran over Harry J's. The gate hung gaping open like a patient in a dentist's chair. Harry J wasn't there. There was a truckload of empty beer and liquor bottles on his kitchen table and a scattered trail of them going off to the field. He wasn't in the station either.

I finally found him wandering down Finn Road, hands in his pockets, staring up at the bright moonlit night.

'Ah, they're juss some kids,' he said, 'some friends of the twins drove down from New York fer the night. Their graduation or somethin'. At their age they need ta have fun.' He was drunk but he was something else too.

I walked with him for a while. He talked about being kids – the days of he and Wendell, then me and he and Wendell. And then me and he. And one of these days just he – the need for a change. The heavy-weighing sadness of realizing you're growing old among old things. Rusting right along with them, nobody ready with the Bondo, the Rustoleum – no Earl Scheib spraypaint you fresh. Not like Wendell. Wendell was smart – despatched in combat still young and showroom-new. Still a kid. I let him talk for a while then I took his hand and I talked about me and he and Wendell and then he carried on up Finn Road. I went back, cursing Wendell again and hating everyone under fifty.

I got to the station just as Sheriff Frobisher did. 'What in hell's goin' on out there,' he said, training his searchlight on the field. It picked up two half-naked figures leaning up against the front of a '74 Chrysler New Yorker once belonged to the Clinton Manor Inn. One was sprawled cross the hood, the other straddling the legs of the first and bucking like those kiddie rides outside the Walnut Creek five and dime. I found myself wondering did the '74 New Yorker come with one of those spring-back hood ornaments. Funny what you think about in a crisis.

'Jesus H. Christ,' cried Sheriff Frobisher, and hauled himself off to the field.

I followed. The scene was mayhem and professionally done at that. Bottles and cans were everywhere, sticking out the uncut grass like mushrooms after rain. Car headlights were smashed, windows shattered. A few doors hung ajar on broken hinges. And inside just about every car were teenagers in various states of undress, legs sticking out one side, heads the other. Some were off dancing in one corner of the field, gathered in a circle around a burning bucket seat. One of those big portable tape players with all the knobs and buttons and lights looks like a 747 cockpit was blinking nearby. The kids were twitching and jerking like Darcy and Marcy did that day at Harry J's. Somebody was screaming and I thought, Oh God there's been a murder, then I realized it came from the tape player. The kids twitched faster when they heard it. Everything looked like one big night at the Somerville Drive-in we used to go to in the '50s except out of control – there was no screen and people were making their own movies. Mostly porno.

I didn't know what to do. Neither did Sheriff Frobisher. He sat down heavily on the ground. 'Jesus H. Christ,' he said. You could see how he felt. He did his share of breaking up rowdy high school parties and fights in the bars after the Flemington Fair but this was different. This was city living come for a visit – a little 42nd Street plonked down in Harry J's field. Sheriff Frobisher stood up and tried not to look around. This wasn't ordinary keeping the peace, this was work for the riot squad.

Darcy and Marcy were nowhere to be found. Which was just as well, because if they were I would've wrung their bratty goddamn little necks. Excuse me, but I knew they were at the bottom of this. I knew they were somewhere plugged in, giggling. I looked over at the De Soto. Two boys were hunched over the hood sniffing. They snorted and shook like bulls in spring. The De Soto's smashed headlights stared blankly at me.

'Milton,' I said to Sheriff Frobisher, trying to check the rise in my voice, 'you're gonna have to do something.'

'I know, I know,' he said in his don't-rush-me tone.

'Because if you don't, I will.' If Harry J didn't care what happened to Harry J, I did.

'All right, all right Hattie,' he said. 'No need to get antsy.' He surveyed the terrain. 'Besides, by rights you shouldn't even be here. This is no place for a woman.'

'The women here seem to think different.'

He hied back to the squad car for his loudspeaker. 'Goddamn Trenton and their goddamn highways.'

It was all over, much to Sheriff Frobisher's relief, very quickly. I stormed up and threw a car blanket over the burning seat. Most of the kids were too drunk or too stoned or too fornicated-out to put up much of a fight. The really gone ones we just stacked like firewood in the back of my pick-up and drove to the police station. Harry J showed up as we were loading the last bunch. To tell the truth, he looked gone himself.

'Everybody have a nice time?' he asked. And 'Where's the twins?'

'Harry J, I'm afraid I'm gonna hafta place you under arrest,' said Sheriff Frobisher.

'Aw, Milt,' said Harry J.

'Well, you're gonna hafta come down the station for questioning at least.'

Harry J looked at me, all sad and confused and boyish. I nodded my head angrily. I guess I was jealous.

That wasn't the half of it. Once we got those kids sober and straight and packed off back to New York ('The comin' thing,' muttered Sheriff Frobisher watching the last bunch pull out. 'Goddamn Trenton and their goddamn highways') the stuff really began to hit the fan.

It came in the way of more city people, only these weren't from New York. They were from smaller bush league cities with names like Tarrytown and Lantana. They appeared 'round the same time Darcy and Marcy reappeared, a few days later, and began hanging around them. The twins' ear-plugs hung from their necks like stethoscopes. Their mouths ran like ticker-tape machines.

It became known that these were journalists, if you want to call them that, from the supermarket newspapers – ones for sale at the checkout counter always carry stories about soap opera stars having extraterrestrials' babies – and one morning while weeding tomatos it all came home to me. Fantastic and unbelievable like those E.T. stories, but true. I dropped the weeder and ran over Harry J's.

'Nah,' he shook his head when I finished. His neck rattled in his open-neck shirt. He'd given up ties altogether. (He'd given up a lot else.) 'I know these kids. I work with these kids. They'd never pull a stunt like that. They don't wanna be famous. Besides, they like me. We got an *unnerstanning*. They're OK. Scope?' He grinned.

'Kids're kids,' I said angrily, 'especially city ones. They like nothing better than seeing how much they can get away with. Mark my words they pulled just that stunt. And now you're gonna have a load of gutter press reporters down here poking into your business. They called them, Harry J.'

'You don't say,' said Harry J. Nothing else. He went to the refrigerator, got out a lite beer, fumbled with the ring pull. He never was much good at arguing.

'I do say,' I continued. 'Harry J, those kids are bored. That's their job in life. To be bored. I've seen them when you're not around. They laze around your place like it's the day after the Fourth of July. Clinton bores them. The country bores them. You bore them.'

He offered me the beer with a grin, a disbelieving grin. And it just grew bigger and bigger until I swear to God Almighty Harry J Walmsley was smirking.

Now I don't say I-told-you-so, especially to a proud man like Harry J. But that very afternoon his smirk got wiped off his goofy face, but good. Two cars with out-of-state plates pulled into the station. Harry J treated them like anybody else – gave them the key to the gate, let them wander round the junkyard a while . . . While they were out another out-of-state car pulled up. The driver came over and tried to talk to me but I told him to mind his own business and go back to where he came and find something truly important to write about, like the Middle East. Then he asked me a lot of personal questions about me and Harry J, and I slammed the door in his fat pink face.

Harry J was in the middle of putting some clothes in an old grip bag when I went by for my daily check-in a few days later. I had those newspapers with me. 'Sex Orgy in Junkyard of Sin' screamed one. It told the tale of 'Harry J Walmsley, fastidious backwoods junkyard proprietor' and how he'd been:

> DUPED – By Lies!
> LOOPED – Into Sex Romp!
> SNOOPED – On By Evil Teens!

Turns out the Evil Teens were none other than Darcy and Marcy, who'd recorded that night with one of those videotape cameras and their friends drunk and drugged OK. The paper called it 'this abominable, amoral, un-American behavior', and below a fuzzy frozen frame of Sex Frolic Couple in Vintage Car ran an entire Sexy Sayings transcript recorded in the De Soto.

'Well, ya know the old saying, don't believe everything you read,' he said, smoothing out his good Sunday shirt. 'I never even set foot in the field that night. That's what I told those newspaper guys. I told 'em we all had a few drinks together en then I left them to their fun. They didn't need an old man tagging along. Juss some kids enjoying themselves I said, harmless really.'

'Harmless?' I was not very happy. 'Those two little monsters – ' but Harry J cut me short by jabbing my wagging finger into the newspaper.

'Look at Wendell's De Soto,' he said, 'don't it look good?'

It didn't but he wasn't really looking.

Later that afternoon, while I was writing a letter to the Editor of the 'Sex Orgy' paper, Harry J appeared in my doorway. He was holding his grip. He stuck a bunch of official-looking papers at me. 'Got some things fer you to sign Hattie,' he said. He had sort of a look on his face, one I'd seen maybe once before, when I gave him Wendell's Navy Bible the day of the funeral. Made me cringe.

He sat down while I looked through them. 'These are deeds Harry J,' I said. 'You're deeding all your land and business over to me!'

'Congrajlations,' he said.

'But you can't,' I fought. 'You need a witness, and besides, you're not dead. You can't will stuff till you're dead. It's not binding.'

'Sheriff Frobisher's on his way here,' said Harry J, 'and I know I ain't dead. This is a business transaction.' He stuck out his hand. 'One dollar please.'

I turned away from him 'cause I knew how he'd look – just like his brother waiting for the train to Fort Dix thirty years ago. Oh God, I thought, I'm too old to cry, break down, rip my heart out and throw it down like a gauntlet. I haven't got the stamina anymore to challenge him to a duel like Wendell. You want to fight so bad, I told Wendell, come on I'll fight you. Out on Harry J's field at dawn and we'll have best of three falls. Or fifteen rounds. Or pistols at twenty paces. Either way it won't matter. Wendell just laughed, then didn't, then the train came.

No. Not again.

Then there was the scrunch of squad car on driveway and Sheriff Frobisher burst in, full of information. He'd just come from Clinton. The d'Levis kids were gone he said, some cable TV channel in New York wanted to see their video. And some of the larger local papers had been calling him. Even somebody from the Newark *Star Ledger* phoned up. And dammit, Newark was practically in New York.

'I think we're in fer another round,' he said, glaring at Harry J.

Harry J shrugged at him, then me. He looked calmer than I'd seen since, well, since before the twins came. 'One dollar please,' he repeated. His look was gone. He was almost smirking again.

In return for my dollar, with Sheriff Frobisher looking shocked over my shoulder, I got the deed to Harry J's house and gasoline franchise; the right to the name 'Harry J's Hi-Class Parts'; all current monies and revenues from the business; the deed to the field and the outright ownership of all the cars in it; all objects of furniture and appliances on the premises; in short, everything but his grip and his pine-scented Wagoneer. And his memories. Had it been anybody else I would've considered it a sound investment.

'Where you going?' I said.

'You gonna leave us ta clean up yer mess?' demanded Sheriff Frobisher.

'My cousin in Ohio,' Harry J said, gathering up the papers and putting them in an envelope marked with my name and a clumsy heart drawn round it. 'Stella. She got a coupla kids. Says they're a real handful. Maybe it's time fer a visit.' Now he was looking that agog way.

'And then?' pushed Sheriff Frobisher.

'And then?' echoed Harry J.

I held my breath.

'Dunno,' he said finally.

So these days I run Harry J's Hi-Class Parts, and believe me, it is just a one-man operation. Sometimes people come by to see the cars, sometimes they come to hear the Junkyard of Sin story, which I always try to put in a more truthful light. I point out Harry J wasn't even there, that he didn't really like those kids, that he was far too sharp to be suckered in by them, that once he gets his business interests sorted out in Ohio he'll be back to set the record straight himself.

Every few days the real-estate developers come round

wanting to buy our properties to build condos for more commuters. (Sheriff Frobisher spends all his spare time writing letters to Trenton.) But although their price is better than fair, I won't sell. Harry's losing his purpose in life's suddenly given me one in mine: to see he gets a fair shake come Judgement Day.

I couldn't do much about Wendell, damn him.

So Harry J's Hi-Class Parts is now a living monument to the Walmsley Brothers' memory, a museum to a rapidly disappearing bit of Americana – 'and that man was perfect and upright, and one that feared God and eschewed evil' – like I found on a turned-down page in Wendell's Navy Bible, which I found sitting under the counter next to the house brand.

Some days I just sit in the forecourt and watch that sign swaying in the breeze. Like today. Wendell used to look from here out at Harry J's, field, all perfectly laid out and manicured, and then at Harry J's squeaky-clean filling station, and then at his brother, hard-working but immaculate in his Flying-A uniform, and then finally at me and wink slyly and look at the sign and say, 'You figger that "J" stands for Job?'

He knew damn well what it stood for.

Headhunter
Hymie Savages
Black CD Price!

Today Joey D'Amato was a one-man party. Savage Black had finally made it to CD! This morning, after five long years on the job at Hymie the Headcase ('check out his prices! He's nuts!') they'd finally let him take a delivery, and when he went to check the shipment, what to his wondering eyes did appear but a gleaming stack of CDs of 'Savage Black'! That fantastic first LP – he rushed through the rest of the order clasping a copy to his hairy bosom, then retired to the staff toilet to celebrate.

The CD looked just like a shrunken version of the album he already knew by heart, as if some rock 'n' roll witch doctor (as the Black themselves set forth on the opening track) had got his mojo movin'. Joey had spent three long years waiting, being frustrated and lobbying, 'Dear Mr Trump, being head of a big company like Dynamicorp you probably don't know that Dynamicorp's record company Everest hasn't put out the Savage Black record 'Savage Black', the *first double platinum record ever in the history of Everest*, on compact disc yet. Being a frequent buyer of Everest records, also a faithful Savage Black fan, I feel this is not good for your business.' His efforts had finally led to this – unrestrained euphoria while Phil the Assistant Manager pounded on the door and shouted, 'Joey, we're sixteen copies short of Whitney Houston – what the hell've you done with the goddamn purchase order?'

Naturally when work was over a formal celebration was called for. Not a big one, because Mary was working the late shopping shift at the drive-in bank and needed him to go around to her mother's to pick up Darren. But a celebration none the less. With a new father's unerring sense of nostalgia, Joey turned the secondhand Toyota into the parking lot of the Dive.

Inside the Dive it may not have been 1975 but it certainly wasn't far from it. Jocko the proprietor and sole employee had never seen the point in decorating a bar a) so dark you couldn't see anything anyway, and b) where you only came to drink yourself off your bar stool. To that end he occasionally swept the floor. That had been it, for the past thirteen years.

'Hey Jocko,' greeted Joey.

'Hey yerself,' answered Jocko. He may or may not have known Joey.

Joey pulled up a bar stool and tossed his prize on the counter with an air of careful casualness. Garry Shane, Savage Black's well-padded wildman leader, snarled shrunkenly at him. Joey snarled back. Felt just like old times, like back in high school when the Record Time was next door and he and his crowd used to rejoice over the latest Black and Led Zep. and Skynyrd at the Dive. Before Jocko got busted for underage drinking.

'Gimme a depth charge, Jocko.' It fitted the mood.

'Unh,' said Jocko. He filled a filmy glass three-quarters with beer, then sank a shot glass of whiskey in it. He handed it to Joey who, just like old times, attempted to knock it back in one.

'Must be gettin' old, huh Jocko?' he bantered when he'd finished choking.

'Erm.'

'Must be my reflexes slowin' down. Used to be able to do that in one, Jocko.'

Jocko didn't reply.

'Yep . . . used to do it in one. Yep. One.'

Jocko went around back. Joey fingered his shiny CD. After a while he leaned over the bar and shouted, 'Any chance of one for the road Jocko? Just a beer I mean.' Jocko reappeared. 'Yeah, just a beer I guess. Gotta pick the kid up from the mother-in-law.' Joey thought. 'Better make it a lite beer in fact.'

Jocko brought a lite beer over. Joey thought he looked at the CD as he slapped the beer down.

'Remember these guys, Jocko?' He held the CD in front of Jocko's face, Joe Friday displaying a mug shot.

'Nah.'

'Sure ya do. They used to play around here a lot before they got big. Used to play the Arrow Lounge in Plainfield. They might've even played here, before you had the place. When it was the Come On Inn.'

'Still is the friggin' Come On Inn.'

'They got real big ya know.' Jocko disappeared around back again. Joey raised his voice. 'Real big. First double platinum album ever for Everest Records. In '75.'

No indication of life, let alone attentiveness, emanated from around back. Joey raised his voice further.

'And now they're finally on CD. Took bastard Everest three years. But they're finally on CD, ya know?' He was practically shouting. 'Finally.'

'Will ya shut the hell up,' Jocko yelled from around back, 'I'm only around back, I'm not in friggin' Alaska.'

Joey felt a little stupid. And Garry Shane looked like he was laughing at him.

When Jocko reappeared Joey decided to change the subject. 'Say, where is everybody anyway Jocko? Hey? Where's the party, man?'

Jocko jerked a thumb towards down the road. 'Casablanca,' he muttered.

'What, that gaybo cocktail joint? The one with all the plastic palm trees? Come on, what about Bernie and Nick and Haybone – you know, those guys? My crowd?'

'Casablanca!' Jocko exploded. 'En ya know why? Cos now they all married they don't want no depth charges, they don't want no rock 'n' roll glamor-boys, all they want's some high-school tail that put out en don't give 'em no lip, en that's where all the high-school tail is!' He glared at Joey. 'So what the hell *you* doin' here?'

And Garry Shane looked like he was laughing at him.

At Mary's mother's Darren was upstairs asleep in Mary's old cot. Joey brought the CD along to show Mrs Ashley. She loved hearing him talk about technological innovations. She herself had a state-of-the-art VCR, a beautiful Japanese model Joey had bought on employee discount at Hymie's, but she complained there was nothing on TV worth taping and none of the films at the video store seemed to be made with her in mind. Still, her eyes had sparkled when Joey came around to install it, and she asked him so many questions he felt like an expert on a call-in program.

'She does that,' Mary had told him once during an argument about his inability to advance at work, 'because it makes her think you're getting somewhere in a hi-tech industry.' Mary, of course, knew better.

'Looka this,' Joey whisked the disc out of the case before Garry Shane could snarl at his mother-in-law. He wondered wincingly if she remembered the Black from his and Mary's teenage days. 'It's one of those compact discs I been tellin' ya about.'

'It's very small.' Mrs Ashley was looking that befuddled yet fascinated way she did when she wanted to hear more. Her fingers fiddled with her sweater clasp. Joey's chest puffed out.

'Yeah, but it's got a whole album on it.'

'Who's that on the cover?'

'See?' Joey hurriedly stuck the disc in her face. Her glasses became two glinting saucers of silver. 'See the tiny grooves? That's called laser-etch technology.' Laser was the buzz word, he knew. His mother-in-law still considered lasers strictly Buck Rogers territory.

'Wow.' She took the disc from Joey gingerly and historically. Thomas Edison's mother-in-law holding the light bulb. 'It's so light. Lasers. Amazing.' She switched the disc to her other hand and dangled it from her earlobe and giggled. 'It'd make a good one of those kooky earrings, wouldn't it Joey? The kind Marybelle would like, the kind I wouldn't let in the house when you were teenagers. So big and gaudy,' and she removed it, frowning slightly.

Joey went upstairs to get Darren, hoping Mrs Ashley hadn't smelled the alcohol on his breath. Even though Mary earned as much as he did (more, when you included late nights like tonight) he liked to think of himself as the provider, particularly when dealing with her mother, who had told him when they'd married she expected great things from him. Going to the Dive was not one of them. 'I'm sure Mr Ashley is smiling down on the both of you somewhere,' she'd said.

He was probably scowling, the interfering old bastard. He and Joey had never got along, especially on those swampy summer nights Joey used to roar up in front of Mary's house in his convertible Blackmobile, the Black blasting from all four speakers. The old man used to turn the most psychedelic shade of purple – like Garry Shane's flares, Joey once pointed out to Mary. She was a Savage Black fan too (wasn't everybody?) but didn't appreciate the comparison.

'It was a *compliment*. Jesus, Mare.'

'You know about his blood pressure. And his ulcer. Can't you turn it down just a bit?'

But Joey always forgot; the Black were like that – got under your skin and made you do things you shouldn't. It was the drumming, Joey reckoned. And all those raucous rampaging songs Garry Shane sang. Thanks to him Joey carried a substantial burden of guilt over Mr Ashley's untimely death, even though the doctor had said it wasn't related to his blood pressure or his ulcers.

And good riddance to him too Joey thought as his feet sank into the deep pile carpet of old man Ashley's bedroom. The next second he crossed himself and apologized out loud, a practised maneuver.

When he looked in at his son Darren's eyes were open but unmoving. Joey hovered over him impatiently, eager for the day Darren would finally recognize his own father. So far nothing but quiet drooly grins, which annoyed Joey with their smugness. Still, he was a good kid; behaved himself with Mrs Ashley, and usually let his parents sleep through most of the night. Joey kept a kid-sized baseball glove in a corner of their condo and regularly worked it over with Glovolium to keep it supple for that red-letter day Darren would use it. Mary never failed to shake her head when she saw him doing this, and mumbled about how he could keep his mind on some things so remarkably well. She answered his protestations over the months with a fifty-fifty split between bemusement and frustration.

'Hey Bambino,' he called softly, using his own father's nickname for him, 'hey. Ya ready to go?' Darren still stared unnaturally. 'What're ya, daydreaming? Now what could you possibly have to daydream about?' He looked to see there was no one else in the room. 'Mother's milk? Hey? Bambino? You and me both.' He grinned. But still nothing.

With that unique tremor of terror which rocks new parents whenever their infant acts in a way not covered by the book, Joey dived for the crib. He fumbled in his jacket pocket for his keys but instead pulled out the uncovered CD. He waved it in the air over Darren, who erupted into burbles and punched at it with baby roundhouse swings.

Joey sighed. He wiped his forehead. He'd read not long ago that Garry Shane had had kids back in '75, and one of Mary's women's magazines recently did a cover story on him, 'The Sexiest Grandpa in Rock 'n' Roll'. Had he worried about his kids dying? How could he have sung all those songs about freeing young girls with his tower of power while his own children in smelly diapers were wandering around backstage? Darren suddenly snatched the CD with an arm like a tentacle and started drawing it towards his bubbly mouth.

'Whoa,' said Joey, prising the hooked fingers from the precious laser-etch technology, 'hold your horses Bambino.' Darren's determination and strength had appeared out of nowhere a few weeks ago, along with an attendant desire to ingest everything within reach. His parents found themselves registering previously uncharted tremors of terror. 'That's the greatest band in rock 'n' roll you're trying to eat there.'

The thought of that made him laugh; he'd have to tell it to Mary. 'Obviously he's got good taste,' she'd say, always good with a comeback, and they'd both laugh and he'd mix her another cocktail and feel very grown-up indeed. Joey liked the double-edged feel of that – the maturity he'd been chasing all his adolescence finally brought to bay, and him as father sharing a private moment with his wife. Something Mary's old man never believed could happen.

Downstairs he paused for Mrs Ashley to coo a wavey-wavey farewell at the jumble of flannel and playsuit in the baby basket. Then he waded through the ritual agonizing inquiries about his work – how soon before they put him in charge of buying, how soon before he was transferred to that beautiful new Hymie's in the Route 22 mall . . . Joey answered in his best hi-tech provider's voice, all the time crossing and apologizing in his head. He left with both his mother-in-law beaming and a carton of his favorite expensive ice cream under his arm.

However, as he was pulling out of the driveway, at last exhaling freely, Mrs Ashley came banging out the screen door.

'You left this,' she said curtly, thrusting the Savage Black case through the open window. Garry Shane, his permed bleached mane raging around his head, his leopard-skin pants gripping and bulging obscenely, was laughing at her.

Joey halted in mid-exhale. He looked up.

His mother-in-law was frowning. 'That's that same awful group isn't it? Oh, Joey.' Her brow was laser-etched with grooves. 'I thought you'd given that horrible noise up ages ago. I thought you'd grown up. I thought you were going to get promoted out of that ghastly record section. I thought you were going onto the home computer counter. I thought . . .' Her voice faded out like Garry Shane's at the end of 'Rock 'n' Roll Witch Doctor' then faded back in with a teary refrain: 'Oh Joey, if your father-in-law could see you now . . .'

The celebration crash-landed with a roar. The bitter nostalgic smell of burning rubber settled in Joey's nostrils. In the basket beside him his son was screaming, the way the Toyota's back wheels just had on old man Ashley's driveway.

It was a long patch, one that wouldn't soon fade away. One that would have done the Blackmobile proud, one that made him feel quite sick.

A Barn Razing

'That's not the point Doris,' said Tarkington Spengler's father to his good wife over the dinner table. 'The point is we've got the Nips on one side of us, the Canucks on the other, and the Limeys and the Indians waiting in the wings.'

'Well, that's fair enough,' murmured Tark's mother, sandbagging her mashed potatoes against him. 'After all, it was originally their land. If anybody has a right to it, it's them.'

Tark's father stopped in mid-explanation, patiently embarked on another one. 'Not that kind of Indians, sweetie. Indian Indians. From India.' He tried to come up with the right word but couldn't. Indian Indians were still too recent a phenomenon. 'You know – Gandhi.' Doris didn't acknowledge. 'Erm – Mrs Gandhi.'

'Gunga-din!' cried Tark, hoping this was the right thing to say. He'd recently seen the movie on Saturday morning TV. He wanted an elephant.

'That's it, Tarkie!' His father gave him the benefit of recently recapped teeth. 'Gunga-din!' He chortled. 'Wait'll I next bump into those Patel brothers!' He smacked the flat of his hand on the table.

Tark smacked his hand on the table too. It hurt. 'Pretty good, huh Dad? Pretty good! And I thought of it. Right, Dad? Right?'

'I know which Indians you mean,' said Doris. She shot her son a look. He immediately felt like he'd just wet his pants. Something he hadn't done for years.

'I don't know why you just didn't say so then,' muttered Tark's father. 'You're always doing that. Waste of everybody's time.'

Tark's mother lined up the rest of her meal behind her potatoes.

'So like I was saying,' Tark's father took a piece of meat, masticated, banished it to the back of his cheek, 'just converting the barn into residential units isn't good enough. Sure, we could get a fortune for 'em, but you know what the Nips and the Canucks and the Limeys and – ' he flashed his teeth again at his son, who jerked straight up in his chair – 'the Gungas want to do?'

Again his wife didn't acknowledge. She was focusing on a point in the air just past her husband's cheek.

Tark looked hard at his mother. Still nothing. He turned and blurted, 'What do the Gungas want to do, Daddy?'

'Well, I might as well tell you Tarkie,' his father leaned conspiratorially towards him, 'since your mother seems to be banished to the bog.' (This was something Tark's grandmother had sometimes threatened his mother with when she misbehaved as a girl. And one day, when Doris Tarkington and young Mr Spengler from inland were out walking across the wild stretch of bog behind her house, she burning with so much to tell, she had revealed it to him. Young Mr Spengler thought it hilarious. And when he was older he found it handy for explaining the escalating silence of their married life.) 'The Gungas want condos. If they had this land they'd knock that old carriage barn down quicker than you could say "Bombay Away", and cover the whole site with low-cost, high-return condominiums. It's what the Nips and the Canucks are already doing out at Pelican Point.'

'On land that still hasn't been cleared for development in the courts,' said Tark's mother.

Tark's father retrieved his cud and resumed chewing. 'So what? By the time it gets through you've got maybe a hundred and fifty units already built, maybe seventy-five sold, and if you're lucky, a few inhabitants – ' the beach-white of his teeth sinking under a flotsam of half-chewed food, ' – what're the Nips and Canucks gonna do then? Say to the government, "Yeah, OK, you win, we'll put it all back"?' He swallowed abruptly with a grunt. 'Get real, Doris. This is the twentieth century. Those companies invested with huge extra funds just to pay the fines they knew they'd incur.' He smirked. 'Or whatever. They planned on breaking the law.' He trawled his fork around his plate for any remaining meat. 'With all these *pree*-servationists and hysterical historical types screaming blue murder these days, they got to. That's just business.'

He turned to Tark, who was probably old enough to start learning about business. 'Your mommy thinks building houses for people is like playing in your sandbox. Isn't that silly?' Tark nodded vigorously. 'Now just imagine you're in your sandbox with all your toys, making roads and houses and everything . . . and with me so far?'

Of course Tark was, but he didn't play in his sandbox any more. He was much too big for that. He wanted to point out to his daddy how grown up he'd become but his daddy didn't want that. He bit his tongue and nodded his head.

'So there you are, making your little toy town.' Tark's father etched a scratchy blueprint in the gravy on his plate, leaning extra hard on his fork at corners. 'And if you don't like it, you can just clear it away and start again.' He swooped down on the blueprint with an avenging angel of bread. 'Just like that. Whammo. Your mommy thinks real life's just like that.'

'Shut the hell up, Ellsworth,' said Tark's mother.

'And she swears too, Tarkie. Tsk, tsk, tsk. Time to banish her to the bog, I think.' He winked at Tark, who flushed and gurgled back.

Doris threw back her chair and left the room.

'AND WHILE YOU'RE OUT THERE,' Tark's father roared after her, 'YOU BETTER BEAR THIS IN MIND – I'M GONNA TEAR DOWN THAT FRIGGIN' BARN TOMOR-ROW WHETHER OR NOT I GET YOUR OLD MAN'S PER-MISSION, AND NOT BECAUSE I WANT TO, BUT BECAUSE I'LL BE DAMNED IF THE NIPS AND CANUCKS AND FRIGGIN' LIMEYS DO IT FIRST!'

Her reply was a storm of slammed doors. Tark didn't know there were that many in the house. Ellsworth glared at the only one remaining open, the one out of the dining room. Only gradually did he become aware he wasn't alone. Finally he said, more to himself than his small son: 'You'd think she'd be more patriotic.'

'It's not fair. You need some kind of stability around. A real home. You're still just a baby.'

'Am not. Babies . . . babies play in sandboxes.'

Her long smooth fingers reached down and tussled his hair. Fine and straight like dune grass. Like hers. 'Of course. I forgot. We're going to have to give that sandbox away, aren't we?'

For Tark, outgrowing things was still strange. 'We don't hafta *right now*, do we?'

'Of course not.' His mother's laugh, a sandpiper skipping across the bog.

'So what did Grandpa say?'

Doris sighed. It really wasn't fair. If only her mother were still alive – there was something about men of her father's generation. You just couldn't talk to them about emotional things – love or unhappiness or divorce – every-thing had to be ledgerlike, balanced, businessed. Then they were fine. She'd told him in terms he could understand: the old barn, if dismantled, could fetch approximately 5,000 dollars for the wood alone, which young city people (faddish acronyms would be lost on him) would pay dearly for. Rustic Seaside America was very much in vogue these days.

Why? he had asked. It's salt-stained and shot through with wormholes.

He was retired, living in Florida, content with war history books, news of his grandson, and tinkering with the wheezy air conditioner he'd bought when he moved out. Exactly, she'd answered. Evidently they can't make wood like that in the factories. And nobody wants to wait while it gets weatherbeaten. Nobody's got the time. But everybody likes the effect. Reminds them of the old days when life was simpler.

A load of hooey, he said.

She laughed.

There was a crackly pause. How much for it again?

She felt her heart sink. 5,000.

And that's all he needs to secure the loan to start the development?

Yes.

And you're sure all this'll get him out of debt, once and for all? And get folks talking to you again?

Yes.

No life was ever simple. Pull it down.

'Grandpa said it was OK.'

Tark said nothing, just moved slightly away, pretending to be interested in something on the ground. Doris watched him. A year ago news like that would have sent him into a sobbing fit of loss; two years ago he would have been too afraid to park his first bike in the barn because of ghosts; in a year he'll have trouble remembering what the barn even looked like ... Things were happening too fast, mirroring Ellsworth's latest effort to transform her history into money in the bank – itself coming on the coat-tails of a foreign-backed development boom so quick, ill-conceived and explosive it had already cleared several planned community-sized kill zones in the heart of her home town. Which in turn had opened the way for the invasion of chipboard Victoriana currently surrounding, sieging and slurring her great-grandfather's house.

'Know what?' said Tark squinting up at her.

'What?'

'I'm gonna sleep in the barn before it goes. Tonight. I'm gonna go upstairs into the junk loft. I'm gonna say goodbye to it.'

'What about ghosts?'

Tark fixed her with a witheringly patient look. His father over the dinner table. 'There's no such thing as ghosts.'

But to be on the safe side, Tark wore his Ghostbusters T-shirt. Which was a good idea because in the gloaming the barn looked . . . *pissed off* was the word older kids at school used, all dark and glowery and brooding. His mother looked like that a lot, particularly when his father was on the phone to his inlander backers, his voice drilling across the room in its flat nasal inland drone: 'Hey there Aaaaal, howyaaaadoinnn hehhh, how's life in the big baaaad citehhhhhh?' Tark could mimic it almost perfectly; his father thought it hilarious. His mother glowered.

But it was really her own spirit Tark knew he could depend on. Her stories of a childhood spent burrowing through the Tarkington memorabilia of the junk loft; her memories of the Friends of Nature club with Katie and Tommy and Franny from the Christman's farm down the road, and later the Boy Hater's Club, with just Katie and Franny and their little sister Baby Babs (who they all decided was too young to join but who was let up into the loft anyway, solely for the purpose of taunting) and, much much later when he had ceased being Mr Spengler, her first clinch with Ellsworth. Doris had never properly explained what a clinch was – each time Tark asked she scratched her head and frowned and came up with a different answer. It's a dance. A board game. A drink – half a shot of passion fruit, topped up with a crate of bitter lemon. That last one always made her snort, although the thought of his parents dancing around the decaying Tarkington relics did it for Tark. He wasn't sure why.

Inside the barn was redolent with smells of straw, oil and ancestry – ghostly whiffs of horses, flivvers, and salty

Tarkington ages. The floorboards were arranged in long narrow strips held down by spindly spikes – unlike anything Tark had seen in the Pelican Point beach development, where most of the kids he now knew lived. In places the floorboards had warped with age and curled upwards, looking like the toes of elves' boots in the fairy tales his mother read him once upon a time on the old Pelican Point beach. He knelt beside several and from underneath retrieved the booty of an equally fairy-tale boyhood: a necklace of pointed black devilfish egg cases, several monstrous-shaped pieces of driftwood, an olive jar crammed with jewels of smooth washed-up glass. Copies of coded messages and treasure maps sealed in empty bottles and hurled into the sea. Several moldering shoe boxes of magic shells. A piece of packing crate swarming with Oriental characters which must have floated all the way over from the mysterious East. How excited she'd been when he'd shown her that! Tark carefully gathered everything up, and sighing the way his mother used to whenever she reached the end of a favorite fairy tale, mounted the creaking steps to the junk loft.

At the top of the steps Tark flopped into a ragged wicker chair. He put the egg case necklace around his neck and reverently deposited the rest of his treasures on their favorite spot, a workbench his grandpa had made from an old crabbing dory. He tested the air with another sigh.

From the front window of the loft he saw a light snap on. It was coming from the attic of the house – the old office his father used to wheel and deal from the days he wasn't off wheeling and dealing in the city. The place where, several years ago, the news had come that the biggest wheel and deal had fallen through. The bog wouldn't drain. The Anglo-Dutch company Ellsworth was wooing had decided that too much had been sunk into it. Literally. It would never be solid enough to take foundation pilings – and Spengler Development hadn't informed them of this. There would be legal proceedings. On that occasion Tark had watched his mother drag out his father – soggy with the house brand he kept for celebrations and raving against the Clogs, the Limeys, the water table, the goddamn ocean – and lock the attic door. It had remained locked for a long time following the bankruptcy, until his father discovered town houses – which didn't really even need foundations. Which could just as easily be slapped over a couple of feet of landfill. The attic door was thrown open like the Holy Door of St Peter's, the old debts sweet-talked, and Spengler Development was back in business.

Which made Tark feel very important indeed. Other kids' dads mowed the lawn or went bowling or watched the big game on TV, his dad raced into the city and staggered back out, trailing papers and plans, smelling of smoky rooms and bitter drinks. Tark imagined him in inlander's city attics, clinch in one hand, fat cigar in the other, breezily quoting things far too complicated for little boys to understand. This thrilled him.

Tark pressed his face up against the loft window. The attic door opened and his mother entered. Tark held his breath; was she going to drag him out again? She approached his father as he sat hunched over his desk, her arms folded and hugging slender shoulders. She unwrapped them long enough to point out at the loft. Ellsworth got up, put his arm around her, bent his head towards hers. She shook him off. He stormed around to his desk, leaned on it with his knuckles, like a soap opera tycoon. Doris pointed again to the loft. Ellsworth pointed to the open door. They carried on like that for a while, like wind-up figures, until his mother finally ran down and out. His father slammed the door behind her. He went to the window. He must see me, thought Tark, I'd better wave. He began to, slowly at first, then more fiercely. He must see me. He must! He must! Daddy! Daddy! LOOK!!

Ellsworth sat down, his back to his fortune and heir, and pulled out the bottle of house brand.

Disappointment flamed in Tark's blood. Then it died, leaving him shivering. He tried to recall his mother's stories.

Things would be a lot better if she were here right now. Fumbling, he unrolled his sleeping bag. He arranged his treasures in a hasty halo around him; it was night and he was alone in a dark creaking place.

'What the hell are *you* doin' here?' A semicircle of men's faces, some accessorized with shoulders, pickaxes and sledge-hammers, assaulted Tark. In the middle were Ellsworth's bloodshot eyes and glinting teeth. A crowbar protruded from one fist, raised at his son.

'Well?'

Tark groped. 'I – I was camping out, Daddy. For the last time. Here.'

'Does your mother know?'

'Oh yes. She said I could last night. She said it was OK.'

'Didn't tell me about it,' grumbled Ellsworth. 'Then again she never tells me anything anyway. Friggin' coastie.' It was an original epithet of which he was particularly proud. 'Friggin' coasties like your mother're all the same. Quiet as the friggin' bognight around here.' He addressed the men. 'Gives me the creeps, believe you me.' They shuffled and stared at their shoes.

Ellsworth remembered there was work to be done. He also remembered what a brainstorm of his this whole thing was – how much fun it was going be to beat the Nips and Canucks and Limeys and Gungas all at their own game. And for money too. Big money. 'OK Tarkie,' he beamed, 'you just run along to your mother now.'

'But Daddy, I want to help. That's why I camped out. To be here bright and early. I'm helping. Please let me help.'

The men grinned. Ellsworth shot them a look. Then Tark. His teeth gleaming chainsaw-like. 'Now listen, Tarkington, we're very busy here. This is very important work. You're too little. You'll get hurt. And your mother would never let me hear the end of it.' He jammed his crowbar into a floorboard. 'Never.' It gave an earsplitting shriek. He grimaced deliciously and licked his teeth.

'Now hang on a minute, Mr Spengler,' said one of the men, 'you're doing it all wrong.' He wore an old college sweatshirt and spoke calmly, like a college professor.

'Yes, don't be in such a rush,' said another. Ellsworth didn't like the way he was standing. There was something un-American about it. 'Remember that board's worth money. What we want to do here is preserve the wood as much as possible.' He was slight and lissome, the kind of man Ellsworth had nightmares about Doris coddling his son into becoming. He could feel his skin crawling.

Suddenly he felt querying eyes on him. 'Sorry,' he heard himself apologize, 'I forgot.' He stalled, clutched, changed gear: 'Course you guys aren't really demolition men anyway, hehhhhh.' Why did the kid stare at him all the time? 'That's right. You're preeeeservationists, right?' What the frig did he want? 'Preeeeeeeeeeservationists. Yuppie housewreckers. Hehhh, that's a good one, that is. That's a friggin' laugh and a haaaaalf.' He leaned heavily on his crowbar and guffawed at the heavens, feeling shored up.

Whatever they were they were fast. Tark and his mother watched from the back steps. Tark couldn't believe that something so big and fixed in his life could be struck down almost as quickly as he with his sandbox towns. His mother looked like someone watching a favorite relative dying of a rapidly wasting disease.

The workmen had relieved Ellsworth of his crowbar and suggested he carry, number and stack boards instead. At first he agreed, but soon discovered the insultingly clerical nature of the work and let it be known resoundingly that when *he* employed somebody they didn't frigging tell *him* what to do. The workmen, purring and whirring machinery high up in the rafters, made no further suggestions. So Ellsworth had taken it upon himself to clear out the junk loft.

Tark was worried about his mom. As she watched his dad pitching the contents of the junk loft through its shattered and gaping windows she did nothing but rock twitchily back and forth, her arms hugging her shoulders. (Tark had made sure he'd rescued all his treasures, even the ones he didn't look at much any more.) When his grandpa's dory-bench appeared prow first in the window Tark himself felt a sickening lurch. He liked his grandpa. The dory balanced perfectly on the ledge for an instant, awaiting orders from a phantom Tarkington skipper, all four ramrod legs oars at the ready.

Tark looked at his mother. She looked like she could blow away in the breeze. She looked over at him, tousled his hair with fingers delicate as brittle stars. Then she smiled and turned away.

'Mommy,' he whimpered, suddenly frightened.

'Shhh,' she soothed, resting her index finger on his lips. He tasted sweat. From deep within the skeleton of the barn came a high, flat, nasal cry. It sounded to Tark like 'Bombay Away'. The dory sailed off over the boundless main.

The Spengler family watched it drifting gracefully and languourously, and when it finally ran aground, striking the driveway with a wrenching crack, Ellsworth wiped his hands on his pants and looked out over his budding boom town and licked his teeth; Doris removed her finger from her son's lips and aimed it, rock solid and sure, at her husband; and little Tarkington hid his face in his hands and bawled and bawled and bawled like a baby, like a lonely grown-up.

When he left with his mother early the next day, the barn lay blanched and dismembered across the driveway like the bones of so many plague victims.

Two Gallons

His tongue was tired for he had been talking all the
afternoon in a public-house . . .
James Joyce, **Dubliners**

'What is Absolutely Tremendous about pubs,' summed up the
Beer Monster over his pint of Winter Warmer, 'is that they
never are the same. Twice. Ever. Each day a new challenge,
a new stimulation, a new set of variables walks through that
door, with new ideas, beliefs, experiences – '

'May we play Hatfield Tunnel now?' interrupted Tall
Bastard.

The Beer Monster ignored him. 'An ongoing, life-affirming
interaction between sentient beings in tasteful, dignified sur-
roundings. There really is no need to be anywhere else.' He
drank deeply.

'You didn't think it was so tasteful and dignified when it
was Rocky's Superbowl Cocktail Bar with the goal posts all
over the place.'

The Beer Monster shrugged. 'Mistakes are a part of change.
They give it a human face. Take beer, for example.'

Tall Bastard sighed.

'The Burton here yesterday was a mistake. Crap. Absolute crap.'

'But you always say Burton is crap.'

'Not so, Tall Bastard, not so. It just so happens I had some today which was absolutely palatable.'

'But you've been on the Winter Warmer all day!'

'Haven't. I filched a swift half of Burton while you were in the Gents. Absolutely palatable.'

Tall Bastard bristled. A breach of etiquette had occurred. 'But you've always said Burton is crap. I remember only last Thursday you said "Tall," you said, "avoid that Burton. It is absolute crap."'

'That was last Thursday. Today it's absolutely palatable. Besides, no beer born of handpump could ever be absolute crap. That is my solemn oath.' He drank down a generous libation. 'Now, are we going to play Hatfield Tunnel?' He knew Tall Bastard could not resist a rousing game of Hatfield Tunnel. Like so much of life, it was something done best, and only really meaningfully, in the pub. Tall Bastard leapt with impatience. 'Yes yes yes yes, Hatfield Tunnel!' He craned his giraffe neck above the packed room. 'Where's the rule book? Who's got the rule book?'

'Behind the bar, I should imagine.' As the word bar escaped the Beer Monster's lips his glass filled the void, the *après*-comma sentence drowned in a sluicing current. 'ESB this time, Tall, I think.' He handed Tall Bastard his glass. 'Fresh glass, if you don't mind. And twenty Woodies.'

Tall Bastard frowned. The Beer Monster had recently been uncontrollably mutating into the Fag Fiend, and of a session twenty Woodbines regularly were sacrificed to his nicotine-burnished lungs. Tall Bastard was concerned for his health. 'No Woodies, Monster.'

The Beer Monster was hurt. 'Crisps then?'

'All right, crisps. What flavor?'

'Roast ox. No – smoky bacon. No – prawn cocktail.' Tall Bastard glared. 'Definitely prawn cocktail. And an ESB.' Tall

Bastard nodded grimly and Lurch-like and threaded his way to the bar.

'NO – chicken vindaloo!' screamed the Beer Monster after him, but the crowd had swallowed Tall Bastard up.

He returned agonizingly later with two foaming pints of ale, two packets of crisps and a London A-Z street guide. 'It's a griffin up there,' he said, dumping everything on the table.

'Feudal Christianity imposed its ideals on the Magyars as something superior to their own social order,' rejoindered the Beer Monster.

'Eh?' Tall Bastard stalled, waggled the clutch. 'What are you on about?'

The Beer Monster looked contrite. 'Sorry. I thought you were trying to slip in a sly round of Non Sequitur.' The Beer Monster, ever the competitor, was always on his guard.

'Oh.' Tall Bastard laughed, somewhere between a hyena and a sneezing flea.

'So what's this about griffins?'

'On the ESB sign.' He indicated a placard hanging over the bar announcing ESB's pre-eminence among the discerning. 'It's a griffin. I thought it was a dragon or a winged horse or something.'

'Absolutely Tremendous,' said the Beer Monster through a mouthful. 'What are you drinking?'

Tall Bastard shrugged. 'Abbot.' Tall Bastard had a weakness for Abbot.

'Absolutely Tremendous,' said the Beer Monster.

Tall Bastard opened the A-Z and the game began in earnest.

The play was brisk and cunning, as befits a match between two such studied Hatfield Tunnellers. The Beer Monster opened dynamically with a Greenwich Foot Tunnel, countered superbly by an Aldwych Underpass from Tall Bastard. The Beer Monster, mouth full of prawn cocktail crisps, slyly offered Castle Baynard Street EC4, which forced a surprised Tall Bastard to fall back on that hoary old stand-by, the Blackwall Tunnel. In a fierce exchange, Embankment Underpass begat Beech Street EC2 begat the Hyde Park Corner pedestrian crossing begat the bit of the M25 which goes under Epping Forest – and so it continued. Normal for gamesmen of this calibre, searing controversy reared its head but twice – once over the availability of chicken vindaloo crisps, and once over the legitimacy of the bit of Hungerford Lane WC2 which winds under Charing Cross Station – was it truly a public or vehicular right of way enclosed on all sides, as the rules stipulated? When consulted, the rule book made no mention of it, and things looked bleak indeed for Tall Bastard (whose play it had been) until, in an unprecedented show of sportsmanship, the Beer Monster acknowledged its existence, recalling a particularly fluvid piss he had once taken there after leaving the late lamented Ship and Shovel round the corner in Craven Passage WC2 – not a tunnel, but also not listed in the rule book. Here the game was halted, as swift half-time had been called, and it was agreed over several Pedigrees and Double Dragons that a more comprehensive rule book was called for.

The second half opened cautiously, with veteran Knightsbridge Underpasses and Rotherhithe Tunnels and Islington Grand Union Canal Tunnels all being played. Both combatants made frequent use of the allotted number of Refreshment Timeouts (said number previously determined by the Beer Monster as approaching zero on graph z where x = Quality of Play and y = Minutes Between Refreshment Timeouts), viz:

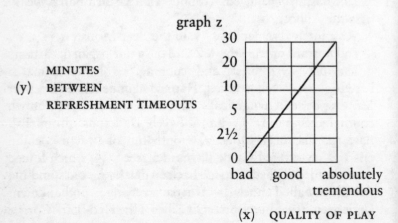

graph z

(y) MINUTES BETWEEN REFRESHMENT TIMEOUTS

bad   good   absolutely tremendous

(x) QUALITY OF PLAY

As the bell was rung by the pub's Time Judge, accompanied by the warning cry of 'Time, please' to let everyone know that the final twenty-minute Lightning Round of Hatfield Tunnel was about to commence, the game looked to be in a deadlock.

But the Beer Monster, sensing Tall Bastard just about on top of zero on the graph, pressed on relentlessly. 'The junction of Robert Street and York Buildings where the cycle shop is.'

'Wherezzat?'

'Covent Garden. By Charing Cross Station.'

Tall Bastard's eyes, two thin red lines across his face, shut. 'Charing Cross Station . . .' His glass in mid-journey flagged in despair. 'Ah . . .' Suddenly it resumed its sloshy progress – 'Ha!' – jerked to his mouth by a brilliant maneuver. 'Underneath the arches!' He grinned triumphantly. He began to sing. 'Underneath the arches, I dream my life away . . .'

'I know the song,' snapped the Beer Monster. Sweet Victory snatched away by an old music-hall number, it was disgraceful. Not in the spirit of Hatfield Tunnel at all. In fact –

' – Foul!' he cried, his final three-pint Timeout erased in one accusatory sweep of his arm. 'Foul! Protest! Disbarment!'

Tall Bastard was still singing. 'On what grounds?' he asked dreamily.

'You can stand at one end underneath the arches and see daylight out of the other.'

'So?'

'So it's not a proper tunnel.'

''S'not?'

'No. It says so in the rules. It says, "a tunnel shall be defined as a covered stretch of right of way one end from which daylight shall not be construed to be visualized, inferred or experienced at the other."'

'You just made that up.' Effectively, now, the Beer Monster had won; Tall Bastard was simply enacting the formalities which signalled the end of the game.

'It's in the rules.' For the Beer Monster had invented

Hatfield Tunnel, and therefore possessed the inalienable right of its stewardship.

'All right then, what about Castle Baynard Street? You can see daylight from either end of Castle Baynard Street, even when it's chock-a-block.'

The Beer Monster's look of supreme condescension and tolerance would not have been out of place in a United Nations conference. 'You seem to forget we were in the Lightning Round.'

'Of course,' Tall Bastard said sharply but resignedly.

'Have you a move? Can you make one? Hmmm?' The Beer Monster sensed Victory again. He began to wriggle.

Suddenly the Time Judge was looming over them, checking his watch and frowning. 'Come on, lads. It's time.'

The Beer Monster became an uncontainable mass of giggly quivering. 'You can't go can you? Can you? Hmmm? *Hmmm?*' He was buzzing like a swarm of killer bees.

Tall Bastard took his final Refreshment Timeout, achieved zero on the graph. In a sense, he had won. 'No. I can't think of another tunnel. Of any definition,' he added a bit acidly.

'Then say it,' chortled the Beer Monster greedily, 'say it, say it, say it, say it, say it.' He was an autism of glee.

'All right, all right. But next time we're playing one of my games. Words With Other Words In Them, or something like that. Something *I* can win.'

'Stop avoiding the inevitable. You've lost fair and square, now take it like a Tall Bastard. Say it.'

Tall Bastard sighed. 'Hatfield Tunnel.'

'O Hatfield Tunnel, glorious subterranean Hertfordshire mistress of the A1, I salute thee with brights blazing, hoorays and huzzahs harking from my high beams – sing hey! for Hatfield Tunnel and know Victory is mine!'

'Shall I get the carry-outs?' Tall Bastard wearily rifled his wallet. It flapped parlously. The Beer Monster was too convulsed in Victory to respond.

When Tall Bastard returned to the playing area, several

refillable jugs of Old Peculiar in his arm, he found the Beer Monster hacking on a celebratory cigarette.

'Divine intervention,' he managed after a prolonged gag, 'I found it under the table. It's not as good as a Woody, it's a Sweet Afton.' He regarded the concerned Tall Bastard through a foggy wreath of smoke – good and faithful and strong Tall Bastard, just like Heathcliffe in *Wuthering Heights*, arms filled and heavy with hops and Yorkshire barley malt . . .

'Two gallons,' said Tall Bastard moodily, indicating at the jugs.

'Absolutely Tremendous,' rejoindered the Beer Monster.

They exited into a London paralytic with possibilities.

I Am Joe's Eye

I am Joe's eye. Just like in the *Reader's Digest*. Of course, as
you've no doubt seen by now, Joe is dead, but thanks to the
miracle of modern technology (and the Eye Bank) and Joe's
girlfried Fern bullying him into getting one of those donor
cards (I can just see her now – 'C'mon Joe, don't do it for
me, do it for the good of humanity, do it for *all mankind*')
I have found a home in the socket of Ted Szczepanski, a
neighbor who used to think Joe was bit of a sissy because he
always dressed pristinely and took precise neat little portions
and never came back for seconds, but who now sees things
differently.

Fern always was a bit of a do-gooder, for ever out and about
helping the poor and saving the whales and what have you.
Joe was a lot more cautious – fitting for the guy who ran the
payroll department in the insurance company where Fern and
most of the rest of the local people here work. He'd go to pick
her up from some meeting or other and there she'd be with her
arms full of leaflets, shouting, 'Joe, Joe you've got to sponsor
me in the bike-a-thon for thus-and-such,' and Joe would half
laugh and half grimace and clap his hand over his wallet

and train me on her in that practiced squint which said, 'Go on – I'm listening.' Whereupon Fern would breathily and stumblingly (I could be murder like that) describe the latest world-bettering fundraiser. Joe would let her get most of the way through, then slowly, slowly draw down my lid, put up his hand to stop her and say, 'Are you really going to go through with it this time?' And Fern would nod her head like the committed world-betterer she was, and Joe would open the door for her and let her in. All the way home he'd have his other eye on the road and me on her, firing off questions about whatever today's cause was:

'That's what the speaker was saying – the Irish must be free to make their own decisions. Without any British interference. He said this all would have been taken care of eight hundred years ago if the British hadn't interfered then, and consistently since. Which is true. So all he wants is some relief money to help the Irish be free. Can you imagine how terrible – '

'Did he say what he was going to do with this relief money?'

'He said they were going to use it to put pressure on the British to leave Northern Ireland.'

'Did he say what kind of pressure?'

'Did he – what a silly question. Did he say what kind of pressure. Pressure pressure. You know, lobbying, letters to the Queen, rallies and pamphlets. Agitprop theater.'

'Guns.'

'Joe, you're so pessimistic, you know that? So cynical. No, he didn't say guns. He specifically didn't say guns.'

'So that means he's not going to take your relief money all the way to Art's Arsenal on Route 22 and ship a giftwrapped cache back to Belfast?'

'Honestly Joe, sometimes I don't even know why I bother. I mean if you're so all-fired cynical about people who are trying, desperately trying to better their lives and their children's, then you might as well let me out here.'

At which point I'd quit squinting, because the last thing Joe wanted was a fight. He just wanted the facts, or as close to them as he could get. He was a facts man through and through, and enjoyed nothing more than engaging me in a good scrutinizing truth hunt.

But he'd still keep me surveying Fern for a bit, because she was known to do things like throw open moving car doors if she thought her integrity was being questioned. She wasn't much for scrutiny. Because of this, because he saw in her the ultimate challenge, Joe was crazy about her. He thought she looked particularly beautiful when she was stewing in one of her righteous rages. I must admit he had something there.

So one day when he pulls up, there's Fern looking more worked-up and beautiful than ever (plus we'd been spending the previous few weeks poring over brochures for romantic honeymoon vacations), and when he opens the door she dives in, throws her arms around him, kisses him so deeply half her face seems to disappear into his mouth. She finally pulls back, and utters those two words which I see even now all the time on TV and in the papers, endlessly attacked in hindsight: 'Squaw's Leap'.

When he's sent the message to stop looking wide-eyed and mock-shocked (and believe me he takes his time) Joe says: 'What about it? It's a very nice corner of Hunterdon County. Out in the country.'

Fern's eyes are bristling with excitement and triumph: 'They want to put a nuclear power station there. Right in your very nice corner of Hunterdon County!'

'Who's they?'

'The government of course! Our friendly, concerned, with-the-people's-best-interest-in-mind government!' No breathiness, no stumbling. Fern thrusts Joe a leaflet. It is dark and bold and crammed with facts. Information belches forth. This is a first – I bug out.

'Hmmm,' says Joe.

Fern takes the opportunity to quote the leaflet practically verbatim, right down to the staggering array of organizations dead set against the proposal, all of whom are going to meet at the site for a mass rally in a few weeks' time. 'I'm going to be there, Joe. This is going to be the biggest thing since the Kenilworth Sewage Works sit-in! They figure more than a thousand people will show up!'

'Who's they?'

Fern shakes her head like a thoroughbred, her mane of hair turning my field of vision spun-gold. She puts an admonishing hand on Joe's thigh. 'Oh, don't be kidding me Joe. This is serious business and you know it.' There is a long silence while I digest the leaflet. Finally Fern can't stand it any more.

'You know how much it would mean to me if you came, don't you? If just once you made some motion – some effort to show you care what happens around you – that you're not an uncaring bigot.'

I can see Joe miffed and confused by this. There are no facts to back this up. 'I'm not an uncaring bigot. I'm not a bigot at all. I just like to get my facts straight, which takes time and delib – '

' – I know that Joe, and I certainly wouldn't allow you to drive me home from all these meetings – and everything else – if I thought you were. But just for once honey . . .'

She's looking particularly beautiful again.

'Sure,' says Joe.

Fact is that all the way back, starting with Three Mile Island, Joe had been gathering information on nuclear power. He'd had a gut feeling about it. And when Chernobyl blew – or rather melted – we had a several-month field day, adding data, sorting through conflicting arguments, ordering an informed opinion. So although the jury was officially still out on this one Joe felt that there was enough evidence to convict.

So it wasn't only because he was going to ask Fern to marry him that he decided to go with her to the Squaw's Leap rally. It was because he'd decided in his heart of hearts nuclear power was not a good idea.

I can still see the cloudless blue sky and the gently rolling field, a hastily erected circle of hurricane fencing slumped around it like a badly blocked hat – and this gives Szczepanski trouble. I mean, there he is, his left eye telling him he's reaching for another ammo clip and his right eye telling him he's actually at that tragic no-nukes rally a while back. Usually he swears, mutters something about wanting his old eye back, cancer and all, and covers me with his hand until the vision goes. But for me it's like staring at the sun – the image of that field has burned itself onto my retina and I can't get rid of it.

Probably because it looked so unlikely, so green and harmless and non-nuclear. When we saw it Joe said to Fern he didn't know whether to storm it or unpack a picnic. She just squeezed his hand and said she was so glad he'd decided to come. I could see the bulge the ring box made in his jacket pocket, as well as the 'Nuclear Power No Thanks' button Fern had made him wear. Joe didn't want to – the way he saw it, there was no point going around wearing your heart on your lapel, especially when everybody else's, bleeding on command like a Pavlov experiment, was just as prominently displayed. But then he remembered the ring, and his father telling him marriage was an equation always in need of balancing, where plusses and minuses didn't always immediately register. He put the button on. I immediately registered Fern's happy approval.

There were a lot of people milling around just beyond the fence, not sure quite what to do, upset about the issue which had brought them all together, getting agitated. I had seen that film *Silkwood*, about the murdered no-nukes woman starring Meryl Streep, on a lot of theater marquees we passed on the way, and Meryl Streep came from not far from Squaw's Leap, so there was a lot of extra tension. Inside, pacing around the enclosure like guard dogs who've just caught the scent of intruders, was a pack of state troopers. Everybody on both sides of the fence was looking a bit jumpy. And of course there were TV cameras from a couple of local stations – big Cyclops-like prosthetics goading everybody on, not there to take things in like me and everybody else's eye, but provoking and artificial.

I saw Joe's hand slip into his pocket while he and Fern were talking to one of her friends, and start fingering his ring box. I was sent a message to scout around the surrounding area to see if there was a secluded beauty spot where Joe could take Fern after the speeches and everything were over, and it was during the course of this that I saw the wire cutters.

They were big – over three feet long counting handles – grey and menacing. One was quite close to our group and when it was taken out and exercised its jaws looked exactly like the snapping turtles Joe was always trying to fish out of the pond behind his condo – glinty-eyed monsters, which every spring gorged on ducklings by dragging them underwater feet first and drowning them, something which made Joe sick. I gawked at the wire cutter, and Joe forgot about secluded beauty spots. He nudged Fern.

'I think we're about to get some action,' he said. The snapping turtle connection had made him edgy.

Fern didn't say anything, but looked excited and abandoned Joe to get the lowdown on the wire cutter.

As with all the real-life tragedies I've witnessed (and since both Joe and Szczepanski were/are keen TV news watchers I know my real-life tragedies) the next set of events was both concatenated and quick. The demonstrators started cutting through the fence at several different places; the state troopers called out through a loudspeaker to desist, that they were vandalizing government property and in danger of trespass; the demonstrators started yelling things like, 'Who killed Karen Silkwood?' and, 'No more Chernobyl', and cut faster and started pouring into the restricted area, where some sat down but more advanced on the troopers, shouting and shaking their fists. The troopers gave up on the loudspeakers and tried to force the demonstrators back through the holes in the fences but the demonstators just kept pouring through; the troopers gave up and retreated to the higher ground at the back of the restricted area; the demonstrators let out a cheer and quite a few began laughing and shouting to chase the troopers. At this point Joe was still outside the enclosure and I was sent looking for Fern. When I spotted her she was halfway up the hill with a cluster of other demonstrators, grinning and shaking her fist and yelling things and advancing on a flustered-looking kid who looked more like a Norman Rockwell Boy Scout than a state trooper.

I saw his arm twitching at his belt, looking for all the world like a nervous *Late Late Show* deputy sheriff.

And a split second later Joe was bolting towards the hole in the fence, and a split split second later I saw the smoke from the gun disperse into that fine blue day.

Only one person had died. I read at Szczepanksi's breakfast table weeks later, Joseph Jones, age thirty-two, was tragically trampled to death as the mob rushed for cover. Of course, it had been a major tragedy, but State Trooper Lefevre was only doing what any state trooper in a similar situation was trained to do – fire over the heads of a potentially dangerous crowd in order to disperse it. These antinuclear campaigners were becoming more than just a cranky lobby group, they were in danger of becoming an organized threat to law and order, I read.

I saw: the hole in the fence, people stampeding towards it and squeezing through it and ripping it wider without benefit of wire cutters; blood; Joe's foot and leg and shoulder and arm trying to squirm through them squirming back through the hole and painfully at odds with them; more people becoming a tentacled mass, becoming stray arms and legs and open mouths and bulging eyes; blood; Joe's arm forced up against me at an unnatural angle; blood; strange hands and fingers and thumbs pushing and grabbing and gouging all up and down Joe's body; sweat; blood; Joe's feet suddenly forced around; feet on Joe's feet; faces sliding to shirts and blouses sliding to belts sliding to skirts and jeans sliding to mud-spattered bare ankles and socks and shoes; blood; sliding to mud; mud mud mud mud mud blood; dark.

For a very long time after that I only saw the afterimage of that field, like staring at the dot on the TV after it's been turned off. Then suddenly it vanished. I felt pressure being released. Light flooded in.

There were people crowded all around me, doctors, nurses, more doctors. I saw a big burly hand raise itself feebly from the bed. It wasn't Joe's. It gestured at the doctors and a raspy voice said, 'Hey, Doc.' I searched up the length of the hand and its arm and then nearly dropped out of my socket – the arm disappeared under a white hospital gown into a shoulder not a foot away from me.

'How's it feel, Mr Szczepanski?' asked one of the doctors.

'It's not in synch, Doc,' came a reply, 'it don't do what my other one does.'

The doctor's glowering face usurped my field of vision. 'Not to worry, Mr Szczepanski. It's just settling in. Happens all the time.' He pulled back, slid his glasses to the end of his long nose and surveyed the scene. 'You must remember we still don't completely understand why transplanted organs act the way they do.' He shrugged a Life's Mysteries shrug – Marcus Welby trying to explain hiccups. I stared bulbously at him.

I saw Fern about three weeks later. Szczepanski was on his way to the county skeet-shooting range, and was en route to Art's Arsenal to get some ammo. He was driving up Balmiere Boulevard, the street her parents live on. Something made me look away from the road off to the right, where I saw her parents' front door open. She was wheeled onto the porch. Her body was wrapped in blankets, but her jade-green eyes flashed furiously. They went straight for me; then something made her wrench them shut and shrivel into the chair. I looked at her for as long as I could; then Szczepanski swore and put his foot on the accelerator.

His skeet-shooting was not as good as he or the boys at the range had remembered. I had never seen a skeet-shooting range. 'Don't worry Ted,' one of them said, 'these things take time. When Jake got his new glasses, took him better part of three months to get his aim back.'

'This ain't a pair of glasses, it's a goddamn eye!' Szczepanski exploded. He threw his gun on the back seat and drove over to the Polish Club for a few beers.

The news was on at the Polish Club, full of the Soviet president's impending visit. The newscasters were talking fulsomely about his *perestroika* and *glasnost* programs, how well they were going, how roundly they were being applauded in the West. There were lots of pictures of him smiling smoothly with various politicians, ending with that by-now legendary shot from his last visit of him shaking hands with his grimly beaming opposite number.

The atmosphere in the Polish Club began to look like that at the no-nukes rally. I twitched a lot. People were ordering more beer, seemingly on the strength of the news report, slamming down empty bottles and calling across the flickering room in English and Polish:

'He shook his hand, you see that? He shook the goddamn Commie bastard's hand!'

'Yeah, and where's that leave us? I'll tell you where – with the same double-dealer who called them the Evil Empire up there congratulatin' him like he's just won the friggin' lottery!'

'We have been sold down the river once again my friends – the Mississippi, the Volga . . .'

'Long live the *Wisła*! Long live Poland!'

Szczepanski grunted, ordered more beer, drank it, left.

Later that day he was in his basement, in a moldy armchair next to a small Virgin Mary shrine. At the Virgin's feet leaned a creased black-and-white photograph of three young men in Polish military uniform. They had their arms around each other yet were smiling stiffly and uncomfortably for the camera. There was an inked circle around the one in the middle, and in the same ink on the bottom border a scrawled message in Polish, beneath which in different ink and a spidery feminine hand was the translation: T. on leave in Warsaw 1939 – love you and miss you terribly.

Szczepanski had a bottle of something – clear liquid with

pictures of peppers and Polish writing on the label – in his left hand. In his right he had a pistol, his favorite one he always took to the pistol range, fitted with a silencer. He took a slug from the bottle, squeezed off a shot into a man-shaped police target hanging on the far wall. The target's head had been covered over with a magazine cover of the Soviet president. Even considering my newness to this, Szczepanski was a good shot. Most of the president's head was in pulpy tatters. The floor was rubbled with chipboard and breeze block.

When he ran out of ammo he picked up a slim book and sent me a blurry message to start reading. It was the only book I'd read since joining him, and I'd read it so many times it threatened to blot out the afterimage of Joe's field. It was called *The Katyn Cover-up: Exposed!*, and as usual I started with the Introduction:

Four thousand brave young Polish soldiers sleep eternally but not peacefully in the forest of Katyn in Russia, and though they sleep, their cries for justice ring out throughout the lair of the Great Bear, making it tremble with fear, for it knows they were massacred by Stalin's own bloody hands.

Szczepanski wanted to look at the photograph before I continued, so I obliged:

THE PEOPLE OF FREE POLAND SHALL BE AVENGED OF THIS MISCARRIAGE and shall bait the Bear with the horrible Truth to which these words bear unblinking witness. The whole world will be our audience, and by the time our work is completed they shall be roaring louder in condemnation than all the Bear's roarings of innocence, regret and compensation. *GLASNOST* IS NO EXCUSE – FIFTY YEARS OF LIES MUST BE PUNISHED.

Szczepanski swigged at the bottle, urged me thickly to read on, which I did, in spite of liquor wobbling words. Once again I informed him of the handing over of 15,000 Polish soldiers by the Nazis to the Russians during 1939, the dark days of the dividing of Poland in the Second World War; their subsequent disappearance; the discovery by the Germans in 1943 of a mass grave at Katyn containing the remains of 4,000; the report from the International Red Cross that documents on some suggested they were assassinated as long ago as 1940; the Soviet government's insistence that they were killed by the Nazis in 1943; the Polish government's collusion with this over the ensuing half-century; the Polish people's outright rejection of it; the mounting anger and attendant suspicion of *glasnost*, both in Poland and among relatives of the disappeared throughout the world – Szczepanski told me to stop.

He got up, lurched to the shrine and knelt before it. I was level with the Virgin's crotch until he bowed his head. I watched his bulging knees grinding breeze block shards into powder. He started with a long vow to respect and honor the memory of his poor recently deceased mother by honoring her request that he, like her, devote his entire life to the tracking down, exposure, and execution of his father's killers. Haltingly he pledged to the Virgin his awareness that, like his mother, this would mean endless vigilance and very little time for frivolities, and that the search for Truth was a hard and hidden one. He would give up skeet-shooting. He would strive harder in his job in the insurance company cafeteria – both as testimonial to his father, who had been a cook in the officers' mess in the Polish army, and to his mother, who had had the cafeteria job before him but presented it to him upon high school graduation to help him with his father's veneration – but the rest of his time and money would be spent in rescuing Tadeusz Szczepanski Sr from the deepfreeze of coldblooded and forgotten death. By any and all means possible. In the name of the Father . . . but he got no further than that, just slumped into a ball, kicking the bottle away, moaning Father, Father, Father, Father . . .

I noticed a trickle of water dripping off the left side of his nose. After a while he brought up his left hand to wipe it away, then suddenly froze. He bolted upright and up the stairs into his scrawny bathroom. I stared at his puffy half-wet face, weeping out of the left side, raining curses on me out of the right. He grabbed a razor blade off the sink and I watched it flashing closer, closer – he dropped it, dropped to his knees and shakily finished crossing himself.

Szczepanski watches the TV news like a POW looking for a security lapse. It is full of the Squaw's Leap tragedy, the Chernobyl anniversary, and the Soviet president's call to reduce nuclear weapons. There is no mention of the Russo-Polish commission which has been formed under the auspices of *glasnost* to investigate the Katyn massacre. I stare transfixed at the newsreel footage of Squaw's Leap. There are pictures of Fern, pictures of Joe, pictures of me, craning out from under somebody's dripping armpit with my expression of horror and pain. And anger, at the disorganization of death Joe felt. The film is frozen here and Joe's face circled like Szczepanski's dad while the commentators sigh and commentate on the uselessness of his loss. I begin to glaze over with the image of the field. The TV moves on. Szczepanski interrupts his swearing at the lying Commie murderer long enough to rage against the uselessness of his own goddamn pinko right eye, then suddenly leaps out of the chair, lumbers into the bedroom, kneels at his mother's bed and reaches for something under it. I am left blinking against the dusty polyester bedspread. He grunts with satisfaction, pulls out a small box and lifts from it an eye patch. He swiftly and expertly claps it over me.

Dark.

He needs me at work – not only to help make him better at his job, but also to spoon out the lunchtime zucchini fritters while his left eye is urgently scanning the cafeteria. As I direct the spooning I can see his father's old civilian hip flask protruding from his catering smock. I send a message about this but it is overruled by his conflicting message which wants me to verify if the person approaching the hot meals section is Fern.

It is. She looks better than the last time I saw her, but not much. She is walking with the aid of a cane, stiffly, like a returning war hero. Somebody is carrying her tray. She stops in front of the zucchini.

'Is that him?' she says to the person carrying the tray. Yes, they reply.

'I know,' she says looking straight at me with her jade-green eyes. They soften and look filmy. 'Hello,' she says.

'Hello,' she repeats to the rest of Szczepanski. 'You must be Mr Ted Szczepanski.' I can see she's been practicing – she uses the same accent as people in the Polish Club.

'Fritter,' mutters Szczepanski.

'I want to get together,' she says. 'I – I know we have things in common.' She winces.

'Yeah, I know,' mutters Szczepanski.

'I have to see you,' she says. The person holding her tray is looking uncomfortable. 'Can you come around this evening? It's extremely important.'

I am forced to look down at the mass of fried zucchini. There is one fritter which looks like the birthmark on the Soviet president's forehead. I bulge while Szczepanski spears it repeatedly with the tongs. He collects the shards and dumps them onto Fern's plate.

'OK,' he says.

'You look different than on TV,' he says.

In Szczepanski's basement that evening the six o'clock news has the results of the inquiry into the Squaw's Leap tragedy. There we all are, all over again. The troopers have been cleared of any wrongdoing, the protesters will appeal. Szczepanski is halfway through the contents of his father's hip flask. His pistol is on the table next to him, loaded.

'Loada Red sympathizers,' he hisses as Joe and I once more come into view, 'loada Commie agitators. No respect for the military. Just the same as the Commies in '39.' He reaches

for his pistol and takes aim at the president's shattered head.
'Kill 'em.' He goes for the trigger, stops, clamps his left hand
over me.

Dark.

— Then light. He's dropped the pistol and I am being eagerly
trained on the TV screen, which is promising details of results
of the first ever Russo-Polish Commission investigating the
Katyn massacre of 4,000 Polish soldiers after the break.

I am ordered not to move, not even to blink, during
the commercials for haemorrhoid cures, shaving cream, a
Broadway play about *glasnost* and the arms reduction talks,
a new feminine hygiene spray, and a new car that makes all
the people around it jump into the air. I am beginning to
ache from not blinking. The report comes on.

The commission's investigation has so far been inconclu-
sive, says an Oriental-looking woman clutching a microphone
under her chin the way Joe did as a kid with a flashlight when
he wanted to scare his sisters. The woman is standing at one
side of a colorless cobblestone square. It is raining.

'Polish historians here are fearing another cover-up over
the still unsolved mystery of the murder of 4,000 World
War Two Polish soldiers in the Russian forest of Katyn,'
she reports. 'Little has come out of the commission set up to
solve the mystery, outside of platitudes from both sides about
the need for painstaking research and promises of complete
cooperation. Worried Polish historians and academics fear
this may lead to a reburying of the incident, and have written
to their counterparts in the Soviet Union asking them to speak
out so that at long last the truth may be revealed. At this point
prospects for any revelations, even in this age of *perestroika*
and *glasnost*, don't look very good.' She signs off, and I am
left looking at a piece on the upcoming tour by the Moscow
State Circus.

Szczepanski tilts almost into the television, then slumps
back in his chair. He takes a very long swig and I experience
that by-now familiar blurring. 'Tell ya what it is,' he blurts
after a long silence, 'it's all them no-nuke Commie protesters

stirring everything up. Interfering. Backing up that lying, cheating, murdering Hitler in fucking Moscow.' He directs me towards the Virgin nervously, part in apology, part in confirmation. He pushes me down to the photograph of his father and keeps me there while he gathers up his pistol, swigs the dregs of the hip flask and prepares to leave.

In the rear-view mirror of his car he is staring at me. 'It's you too,' he says thickly, 'you're a spy – a Commie spy right in my own goddamn head.' I notice how bloodshot and haunted both I and his left eye look, at odds with the grim set of his wide jaw, like poor Joe peering out from that TV armpit. 'The only cover-up's gonna go on around here is you,' he says. He produces the patch, slaps it on sloppily, changes gear like ammo clips.

Out of the bottom of the patch I can see Szczepanski's leg and the floor of the car swaying crazily. Roaring abuse at the Evil Empire and its servants in the land his mother escaped to to supposedly be free, he plugs the gearshift into fourth. The shift roars back and Szczepanski directs his anger towards it. Suddenly the car stops lurching and Szczepanski goes quiet.

In the gathering dark I can just make out the familiar cluster of whitewashed rocks which mark the beginning of Fern's parents' driveway. Szczepanski swears and then I see his foot scuff against one of them, removing a clump of freshly mown grass. His progress up the front walk is erratic and elliptical, and more than once he strays into the thick darkness of the lawn, the bottoms of his army surplus combat boots lost in blackness. He is still raging, although quieter now, and I can't see what he's saying. I begin to spasm uncontrollably. He leans heavily on the railing and I watch his big splayed feet twitching up the front steps.

On the porch his feet are suddenly in light, a spreading shaft emanating from beyond his toes. Also beyond his toes is a stiff shuffling movement, and as I strain to make it out it becomes a pair of mud-caked running shoes.

I've seen them on TV.

'Oh, I'm so glad to see – ' says Fern and then she screams.

And screams. '*What have you done with him?*' she screams. '*What have you done with Joe?*'

'If thine eye offends thee,' gurgles Szczepanski, 'pluck it out.' He giggles. He stops. 'Specially if it's a fucking *Commie* eye.'

'JOE!' screams Fern and I see her bruised, swollen ankles rise up, pulling her heels out of her shoes, which crackle with chipping-off mud. I see the mud and then I see the field, so clearly I blink. Szczepanski receives this and starts roaring again and I feel pressure on me, grappling hands once more as the patch loosens, then slaps back, then loosens –

There is a twinkle at the bottom of my field of vision and I look down and it is Szczepanski's pistol, which he has just pulled from his waistband. It is the last thing I see tilting up, up, and then off-center as the patch is ripped away, and the calm simple serene beauty of the field is all I see, stretching as far as I can see.

That
Motherlovin'
Gauntlet

'Y'all game for Absolution?' That was the best man, whose name I'd forgotten.

From beneath a satin ruffle, the bride moaned. In her lap, the groom brightened considerably. 'Now there's an idea,' he chirped to the bride. 'Best one since I decided to marry you.'

'Since *I* decided to marry *you*,' croaked the bride. She attempted to straighten her veil, which had slipped over her right eye. She missed and smacked herself in the nose. It had been a long reception.

'Whoa,' said the groom, 'y'all see that? She's getting punch-drunk now. Must be all that wedded bliss pourin' out.'

'So is she comin' or what?'

'What about y'all?' the groom said to me. 'Gonna shake them crazy legs all over Absolution?' I'd made a slight spectacle of myself at the reception disco.

No point in letting them know I had no idea what was going on. I reached for the bottle opener as noncommittally as possible. The heart of ole Virginny, to quote the best man, is the heart of the whole durn South – no cardiologist, I. I exhumed a lukewarm beer bottle from the inside pocket of my suit jacket. There are situations where the hiss of an opening beer bottle is as trenchant a comment as any spoken. This turned out to be one of them.

'Knew we could count on you, Crazy Legs,' beamed the best man. 'Now who all else goin' to Absolution?'

You shouldn't fuck with God in Virginia. In a state where churches set up shop as frequently as, and rival the importance of, its other religion, the mall, sticking your nightclub in a punked-out Episcopal meeting hall around the back of town is not a good idea. From the outside, Absolution looked like the victim of an Eastern Bloc party purge: shattered windows taped up with flattened liquor boxes, crumbling masonry, pockmarks the size of bullet holes marching across the façade.

'Target practice,' chortled the best man, pointing at the frazzled neon sign over the door where the cross should have been. 'That's the rednecks comin' down from the hills for a little Satdee night R & R.' I attempted an understanding nod.

What was left of the sign buzzed and flickered like a firefly with its wings pulled off: 'Absolut', then dark, then 'Absolut'. 'J.D. Slammers At Sinful Prices' proclaimed a frayed banner directly below it, also shot up. The best man halted at the heavy oak door and joshed with the practiced *ennui* of a tour guide: 'That sure one holy sign.' His tone echoed yesterday's guide at Historic Luray Caverns: 'And this stalagmite formation we call Snoopy's Doghouse, 'cause it looks like Snoopy's doghouse.' I laughed for the best man, the same way I laughed for the tour guide, and cued my shoulders for the *ennui*-ed backslap.

Inside the Gothic remains of high Episcopalianism had been painted matt black and camped up to Heaven. The bride and groom went straight to the bar while the best man took me upstairs to shoot some hoop. Visions of dirty toilets, dicey syringes and smacked-out Jim Carroll songs commanded my

New York thinking; the best man led me up a flight of stairs carpeted in da-glo Episcopal purple, around a corner and into an open room overlooking the dancefloor; the old choir loft. It had been converted into a games room and was populated by pool tables and stiff-legged unpunk-looking young men who chatted easily, almost relievedly to each other, handling cues like 12-bores. A few open bottles of Mexican beer perched on the tables and a few cigarettes languished in well-tarred ashtrays, but the air hung more country-club clean than juke-joint junked. The balls clacked together discreetly, like change in a collection plate.

In a corner the best man pulled up before what looked like the bastard son of a pinball machine and a batting cage. On the wall at its far end was a kid-sized basketball net. Shooting hoop. He hitched up his pants, licked his lips and looked at me.

'Two years running,' his eyes were shining, and not from wedding reception punch, 'two years running I was highest scorer in the Lynchburg inter-Presbyterian Fellowship League. Y'all got twenny bucks says I cain't hit ten straight?'

I had twenny bucks said I could hit ten straight J.D. slammers. 'Ah – hang on, let me look . . .'

'Never mind,' he rammed an endless series of quarters into the belly of the machine, 'I cain't. Not without my glasses, and they're back at the durned Magnolia Inn.' Three fat orange kid-sized basketballs appeared from nowhere and wobbled down the slope towards him.

If he asks me to go, I thought, I'll have to. Protocol. Despite not having laid unsteady hands on a basketball since high school. 'They're pretty small, aren't they? I'm not really used to – '

'WoooOOOO!' cried the best man releasing the first shot. It went straight through the hoop, swishing testimonial to Presbyterian fellowship. 'Hummin',' he said as he lined up the next one, 'sugah sweet 'n' hummin'.' That went straight through too. The third bounced off the backboard; I flashed him a self-conscious New York Jewish what-can-you-do shrug and wondered if protocol directed that I should buy him a drink. He took no notice, lined up his fourth shot, which also missed. When both of the free shots he got missed as well he swore like a Lil Abner character, all 'gol dingit and dad-blasted'. He dived into his pockets for more quarters. He was three short.

'Y'all got any quarters, Crazy Legs? This here machine just thrown down that motherlovin' gauntlet.'

If I needed an out, here it was. I frantically weighed the change in my pocket normally reserved for jingling. It didn't feel like quarters. I took it out, and was forced to check under the only available light of the basketball machine.

'Nah. No soap, man. Three's a no-go.'

Was this me speaking?

'Two's all I can do ya.' I gave him those. 'Lissen, I'll like book downstairs and hit up the betrothed, OK? Get 'em to cough up and shit.' Was I going on the hyper-Northern defensive or what?

'Shore preeeeeciate it,' the best man drawled, clamping his hand on my shoulder. Was he laying it on respondingly thick? Suddenly I felt like Neil Young in a Lynyrd Skynyrd song. J.D. slammers, my brain cried, sinful prices. That old Underground Railroad to release. I backed out of the games room in a hurry, slavering for sin.

And so it came, the Great Emancipator. I was standing at the bar not with a J.D. slammer but a Manassas Mud ('whups ya once like Gen'l Jackson goin' down then agin like Gen'l Lee on the way back up' grinned the barman, for whom my accent was an invitation to Absolution's sludgelike Yankee Special), afraid to drink, watching the bride and groom twirling dreamily to an amphetamine Billy Idol cruncher, when they wandered into the purlieu of a couple proceeding with the most rhythmic, least delicate, most vertical fuck I'd ever seen.

Well she was anyway. He just looked gaga.

And I felt my Yankee self-control whacked head-on by

deranged, senseless lust. In that pitiable, delirious, all-else-stops way that senseless lust claims its own. (If the act is original sin, then the thought itself is preter-original – even more tenebrously primordial. And lurking. 'Inna mah heart', as the Georgia president once said. And now in the church as well.) My pulse rate soared; my face swamped crimson. My perspective narrowed and focused. My loins stirred.

I was primitive.

'Gentlemen,' I would have said had I been one in this land where so much is still done in the name of good manners, 'you all know what I'm talking about. Ladies, you probably even more.' Dressed in nothing more vampish than jeans, a lumber-jack shirt, Cuban heels and a pair of red galluses crossing like twin interstates above a bountifully fruited plain, she was shimmying buck-assed naked in the eyes of everyone watching, and what's more, she didn't care. No nascent bimbette aping the bump-and-grind-by-numbers of a heavy metal video, no Frederick's-swathed siren performing her bedroom rituals in public – just the unsheathable sexiness of confidence.

I felt my own waning by the second.

The bride and groom swirled by; I pointed her out, rolling my eyes. The groom watched hard; the bride watched the groom. Good dancer, he called hesitantly, then when the bride turned to look, mouthed *go for it* accompanied by a dour look.

I confess I did not; I could not. I was enjoying her far too much already. Her romping curves and streaming hair and roiling, rapturing body were all doing a four-poster mystery dance in my head, and I was not about to relinquish control.

Which is what Chump-change with her was doing; shuffling aside and allowing her to perform the fantasy for both of them. Not my style, personally, and I was wondering if this was the way you advertised for a threesome down here – when she looked barwards.

Hunkered.

Thrust.

And licked.

At me.

And every single thought save one went howling out of my head.

For me – she was out there, ravishing every eye in the place, and it was all *for me*.

I reeled, steeled, glared back.

She came on stronger, touching herself, laughing lightly.

That motherlovin' gauntlet had been thrown down.

The song ended. Chump-change shuffled to the toilets (as per my telepathic diktat), and no sooner had he turned his eyes from her than hers went to work on me. Her look was neither imploring nor haughty nor come-hither. It was a statement, a calm unblinking statement.

So it had been decided. Just a question of formalities now. I relaxed. But my hand was twitching and beaded with sweat as I saluted her with my drink. I bathed my mouth, then went over to where she was sitting.

The music had started up again, a big walloping piledriver of a beat. If rhythm could speak this one would be grunting '*unh*'. Her foot flagellating response; she couldn't keep still. She looked up. Her cheeks were high; her eyes fulgent green. I offered the dancefloor the way a gentleman offers a lady safe passage through a door. She accepted with a look of graceful delight.

We danced.

My God, it overcame me as the beat grunted harder and she flowed response – drawing me in, playing me, intimating – this is all I want. THIS IS ALL I WANT. EVER. And suddenly more desperate: take. I must take. I must possess. I must have this woman, I must capture her, she must do this, always, only for me –

Perspective squeezing, cooling and hardening like volcanic rock; like polished obsidian.

Brutally quickly the song was over – foreplay banished to the same bedside chair as hived-off clothes. Chump-change arrived back from the little boys' room, uncertain. Yet we were not worried; just polite. I released her, glinting with the knowledge that I could banish him again when necessary. She looked at me, that same one of graceful delight. She nodded thanks.

I was not worried. I would have her again.

The best man had come in search of his quarter, seen us on the floor.

'Crazy Legs.' His tone was reverential.

'I know.' My blood quietening.

'More fire in her 'n a roomful of circuit preachers, as my grandpappy used to say.'

I turned to him. Nothing could touch me. 'Sheeit,' I said. 'Sheeeeeeeeit.' I slapped him on the back.

For the remainder of the evening our relationship was a brazen and breathless bout of eye fucking. She out on the floor with Chump-change (now reduced to a fumbling cardboard cutout), hips, breasts, hair an orgy of unsated movement, throat exposed, face languid, emerald eyes triumphant. A pulsing button of sweat at her cleft of breast. I apart at the bar, a swaggering riverboat gambler watching, smiling, approving, savoring the control, the teeming delectability . . . so much so that I felt no compunction about leaving. I retired to the men's room for a few minutes.

During which the music ended, the house lights went up, and as I strode out there was the DJ saying, 'That's all y'all and don't forget your waitress.'

No, not a major panic – remember I was still co-running the world. I searched for my conspiratrix and found her again sitting, sipping a drink, head tilted away from Chump-change's stream of verbal effluent. I approached, set myself leaning against a pillar within eyeshot, and with great satisfaction watched him wander off.

Her head went up slowly, cinematically, her eyes found me right where she knew I'd be. She blinked in the bright house lights; her face clouded over.

I started across the floor to reassure her.

What?

Reassure her?

Talk?

The world was threatening to lurch out of control. What if –

Never mind. We'd made a pact. Fate.

I continued over to her, tried to lean against a chair to look a little less loomy. It squeaked loudly.

She giggled. She was glistening with sweat, her eyes still flashing, but in the light there was something fluttery, almost schoolgirlish about her movements.

It was time to act.

'Uh . . . I . . . ah . . . I really loved your moves.'

Silence.

She lowered her eyes, turned her head away, fidgeted, mumbled, stopped.

Silence.

Explosion: Jesus Christ, she's fucking *SHY*!

Control hit.

She whispered something about liking the way I danced too.

'No, really, I mean it. You looked really . . . really good out there. Very good – listen to me, what am I saying? I mean, incredible. Absolutely incredible. Really.'

She mumbled thanks.

Could this really be happening? Could she really be . . .

What about . . .

Control dead.

I have very little specific memory of what we said, how long we talked (they tell me not long), only that her humility radiated genuine as her gyrations, boundless as her beauty – every bit as desirable, every bit as sexy, every bit as once-in-a-lifetime. And still there before me, warm, wise, motherlovin' wondrous . . .

In other words I was in love. Caring, compassionate, loving love. All I ever want. Love.

Two points for the reversal, a further two for the fall.

And when I finally came to Chump-change had returned and collected her. And squired her out of Absolution and into the clear Virginia night.

Leaving me behind.

Shut down.

Unloved.

The bride and groom sidled up. And the best man, who sought to do the decent thing and revive me with a substantial smack between the shoulder blades, accompanied by a thick wedge of good ole homespun philosophy: 'Don't y'all mind, Crazy Legs, there plenty more hams in the smokehouse.'

I decked him.

And staggered out into the gutter.

No gentleman, I.

Once the Splinter has Worked its Way Out, Where Does it Go?

Here are some more facts, thought Quentin Melrose in the dark of his bedroom: 1) I am alive, it is night and I should be asleep; 2) the only surviving medieval gatehouse in London is St John's Gate in Clerkenwell; 3) I may already have won cash and/or prizes totalling over £50,000; 4) I have always been sexually attracted to interesting as opposed to beautiful women. As he came up with each fact he ticked it off in his mind, but when he had completed the exercise the other list, the list of uncertainties which had been piling up since Sue told him about the baby, was still considerably longer. He wanted to jump out of bed and hop around on one foot banging the side of his head to expel the excess, as he frequently did at the swimming pool, but 5) if I do that it will result in nothing but a headache.

Some of the uncertainties of the list were typical ones of expectant fatherhood: money, fear, doubts about his parental capabilities – those came early on in the list. Later in the list, in fact only several days to several seconds old, were those uncertainites which kept him up at night: if unleaded petrol is so good and beneficial why haven't we had it sooner; how many steps are there in the hall staircase; who is giving my address out to all the junk mail people; am I in love with my wife?

He turned to Sue, looked at her sleeping, swollen form, thought, in my parents' day her condition was considered answer enough. You better love your wife. What's happened – Oh God, another uncertainty. A fact – a fact was needed to offset it. Quick. Quentin was sitting bolt upright in bed now, wincing as though working off swimmer's cramp.

6) I've got 'It Makes No Difference' by The Band running through my head. What a bastard wry subconscious I've got.

Quentin's subconscious actually was no more nor less wry than anyone else's, just at this moment more subversive. Quentin took a vicious pleasure in this. He figured it was just deserts for his uncertainty concerning his love for his wife; 7) for every action there is an equal and positive reaction.

'It Makes No Difference', in case you've never heard it, is about as pure and pained a lament for lost love as has ever been crooned. Quentin had been acquainted with it for years, and for about half that time considered it quite all right, if a bit simplistic on the emotional side. Then his girlfriend, Julia, left him to move in with someone older and wiser, and overnight the song became truth. For three weeks it didn't leave his turntable. Halfway through that period he bought a ninety-minute cassette tape and recorded the song on it eighteen and a quarter times. He spent a long time in the dark those weeks, drinking the advocaat he'd bought specifically because he couldn't stand the taste, listening to 'It Makes No Difference' on his headphones. He moved as little as possible. He wanted Rick Danko to sing *and the dawn don't rescue me anymore* at his funeral, which he hoped would be soon.

Eventually, and much to his chagrin, the dawn did rescue Quentin. And reluctantly he pulled back the nylon curtains of his bedsit, filed The Band back between Ambrosia and Barclay James Harvest, cleared the empty advocaat bottles away and felt the blood limping through his ravaged heart.

Yet for a long time after that Quentin still railed to himself *it makes no difference who I meet, they're just a face in the crowd on a dead-end street*, until one day, in the middle of Streatham High Road, he set eyes on Sue.

After that The Band still careered into his head from time to time, and like an old lover's ring found down the back of the settee, retained the power to make him stop whatever he was doing and sit down heavily. Even though with time Quentin was able to pare the song down to just the last verse, that verse remained the real killer – Rick Danko's lilting, choked confession, *well I love you so much it's all I can do/ just to keep myself from telling you*, followed by the rest of The Band moaning *that I never felt so alone before* – and that, maddeningly, would be Quentin gone for the day. He'd stop talking, jangle his change and gaze out the window. Or he'd smack the side of his head several times, swear and stomp out to the garden. Or hunker deep down into his chair, cross his arms and hiss at Sue just to leave him alone. Sue commented quietly to friends on the upstairs extension that she'd married the world's only premenstrual male.

Quentin was in the kitchenette now, wrapped around a cup of coffee he knew would keep him awake. He lifted it to his mouth and blew on it, allowing the steam to lead him where it would. It wafted him through the kitchenette, hall, and into the sitting room.

There he put the cup down, went to the hall stairs, climbed silently, returned, and sipped thoughtfully: 8) twenty-three, not counting the landing.

But it was no use. The Band had dumped the balance way over in favor of uncertainty. A cancerous knot of loss ate at his insides. His cup jittered. Danko keened. He forced his eyelids shut. The Band moaned. *Have you ever felt so in love with Sue?* He knew the answer. He reached for the telephone, pushed the button with the minicab number. He just needed Julia to stop asking the question.

*

The minicab driver was an unsubtle Turk, and wanted to know did his wife throw him out or was he on his way to see someone else's? Vertiginous Turkish music swirled from the radio and drove The Band from Quentin's head.

'I don't know.' He couldn't remember if Julia had married Mad-dog or not.

'*I* throw *my* wife out last year,' enthused the Turk, adjusting the volume of the radio, 'an' I have fun, fun, fun ever since.' He cornered viciously. 'My brother was catching her with black man.'

'Huh,' said Quentin. They couldn't have got married because if they had she would've let him know (there was still this strange line of communication between Julia and him) and 9) that would have done a number on my heart, opened up a lot of scarred-over wounds and made me miserable. And furious. As far as he could remember he hadn't felt that recently.

'In the launderette. They were talking, laughing. She was flirting. My wife. My brother sees it all. So now I have fun, fun, fun all the time.'

'Huh.'

'You want fun? I know somebody – Irish girl. Big girl. Massage. Cheap. Gets job done, innit? Fun.' He handed over a flower-choked business card.

Quentin skimmed it. 10) Cheap. The driver grinned, turned up the music.

Ted's Fried Clams was still busy, even though it was almost closing time. Quentin looked up at the billboard over the door, a garish mural of a Down East clamdigger proffering a steaming pile of what appeared to be deep-fried droppings. 'From the rock-ribbed coast of Maine, USA' read the floodlit slogan. Quentin looked harder, and clocked a small brass mezuzah over the door. He shook his head. He didn't know much about Maine, USA, but he was pretty sure it wasn't swamped with Jewish clamdiggers. He paced a few yards up the street, thought about hailing a cab home. He paced back. He didn't come into Soho much anymore, and nowadays the whole area looked chain-stored and vacuum-packed, like one of those American-style shopping malls Sue loved to go to. He squinted up at Ted and his clams. 11) I remember when this place was the Coach and Horses and sometimes I'd meet Sue here after work, and it would be absolutely packed out with people. Loud, lusty, living people.

12) I'm definitely getting a cab. I love my wife. This is silly.

The Turkish music chose that moment to whirl out of his head, leaving the way open for The Band to come storming back, which they did, more insistent and world-weary than ever before. Quentin battled, lost, threw open the door.

The sound of the minicab revving outside had wakened Sue. She had hastily thrown on the nearest clothes she could find – Quentin's slippers and worn flannel robe. She now clumped around the house with a glass of orange squash from which she drank deeply, as though it were alcohol, each time she entered a room and discovered Quentin not there. When she arrived at the final room, the sitting room, she found his hastily scrawled note: Couldn't sleep – just popped out for some air – back in a minute. Love you for ever, Q.

Sue read the note again, then a third time. She sank into a chair, the worn folds of the robe enveloping her. In eight years of marriage Quentin had never once told her he would love her for ever. Quentin was a doer, not a sayer. He didn't leave notes. Her belly came up to meet her wide-awake face.

Julia saw Quentin some time before he saw her. She was demonstrating to an uncooperative trainee waitress the art of tying a customer's lobster bib so the customer didn't end up the color of the lobster. The trainee waitress was a vegetarian and an animal rights supporter who approved of neither eating lobster nor the way it was cooked. 'It's the most humane method,' Julia explained, stretching to the limits her reserve of professional politeness. 'Even the RSPCA approve. The lobster hardly feels a thing. It's over in a second. Just like a pinprick.' The waitress grumbled about which RSPCA member had been dropped in boiling water to find out. Julia looked away. The perks of being In Charge.

Still, at least everybody else in this hole seemed to be enjoying themselves, including – Quentin Melrose! Julia's heart didn't exactly leap, but she suddenly did feel better about being Duty Manageress of Ted's Fried Clams, about wearing an absurd plaid pair of clamdigging trousers and a big orlon cable-knit sweater adorned with an adman's silkscreen dream of what Ted himself might have looked like, had he not also been an adman's dream. Quentin had met her when she was just a waitress herself, incapable of getting to work on time and a million miles away from management material. He had become her first serious lover and, as a result, her first serious ex-lover. She had left him ten years ago, upon discovering both punctuality and front-of-house manager Madhat, who had successfully dangled before her the twin enticements of maturity and Eastern mystery. And of course, in moving on, she had behaved very badly to Quentin, but as she'd thought at the time, he's young enough and good-looking enough and well-adjusted enough – he'll get over me. Probably sooner than he thinks.

Julia pulled hard on her customer's bib.

She watched Amelie, the hostess she had trained, gracefully sidle Quentin into the Quahog Corral and order him a drink. She watched Quentin watching Amelie swishing back to the hostess station: the same appraising approval she recalled from all those nights in that damp bedsit, undressing for him by candlelight – it seemed he had got over her.

Then why was he here?

He was married now, wasn't he?

He hadn't looked that good ten years ago, had he?

Her customer gurgled.

They ended up in a basement in Hanway Street. It was a late-night flamenco bar, the only place still open where they could talk. Quentin found himself shouting a lot, but at

1.30 a.m. in London beggars can't be choosers. Not that he was begging – he'd moved on.

To what?

'How are you?'

'What?'

'HOW ARE YOU?'

The music stopped temporarily. Julia listlessly picked candle wax off the heavy Moorish candle holder and rolled it between her fingers. She had untied her hair and it fell the same way Quentin remembered, a safety curtain obscuring the dark drama of her face. 'Fine. Just fine.' The flamenco musicians suddenly threw down a strutting, syncopated challenge, which the dancers leapt to take up. 'And you?'

13) Christ, it's noisy in here. That cosmic balance again. 'Yeah. Great.'

'And how's . . .' Julia's voice dipped below the driving beat. What was her name?

'Sue's great,' replied Quentin. 'Pregnant.' That word found a ride on an offbeat following a heated, stampeding exchange. Sue's condition ricocheted across the bar.

'Oh.' Julia arched one heavy, long eyebrow.

Quentin motioned to the waiter, dredged up the only Spanish he remembered from an unsuccessful Costa del Sol package holiday he'd taken years ago to forget her. 'Dos cerveza por favor.' He'd forgotten Julia didn't drink beer.

'Vino?' she asked the waiter. He nodded. She ordered a bottle of rioja.

Quentin took this all in. She'd always liked drinking, but never by the bottle. He tingled. Maybe she wasn't happy . . .

'And how's Mad-dog?' Tingling.

Julia looked puzzled, then clicked angrily. 'You mean Madhat.'

'What?'

'MADHAT.'

'Oh, yeah. That's right. Madhat.'

Her annoyance snapped at him like castanets. 'You know

how he is. I told you last time I saw you. We split up ages ago.'

Quentin suddenly realized he *did* know; the jilted twenty-year-old in him just wanted to hear her say it at least once more.

'Bastard,' she muttered. She poured out a rio of rioja. The flamenco came to a thunderous, swarming climax.

In the silence afterwards Quentin found he had nothing to say. He watched Julia knocking back the wine. Fast. 'You know . . .'

'You know what?'

'I mean if we'd stayed together back then – like, if you'd stuck it out with me – I could have, you know . . . helped – '

Something was going to be said.

14) And Oh God, the Band are the soundtrack.

Julia leaned forward, filling the space around him. She pushed her hair back. She might be going to kiss him.

'Helped what?'

She had joyfully torn off her sweater as they left the restaurant, and was now dressed only in a man's button-down shirt and her absurd clamdiggers. Her top two shirt buttons were undone, and as she leaned towards him Quentin saw, nestled in slightly damp, perfectly spaced cleavage, the shining beacon of his lost love.

He went to touch it.

It was a small, round, tear-shaped pendant of polished jet, black as her hair, her eyes, the depths of her soul he'd tried first sentimentally, then stoically, and finally desperately to light.

The summer they were in love Quentin and Julia had spent picking grapes in the south of France. The sun had been carefree, the pay abysmal, and he had spent most of his wages on the pendant and necklace he'd found on a day trip to Nice. He had paid out the paltry notes slowly and individually, savoring the transaction with a lover's pride. When he returned it was late. He led her out into the fields at midnight, clasped the necklace on her, and as he molded her moonlit breasts around it observed the full moon tickling the stone, like half-spoken words in a lover's ear.

Her hand intercepted his. She had been watching him. 'Yes, I still wear it. It's still beautiful.' She placed his hand gently on the table. 'I've always thought that. It's about the only jewelry I do wear.' Her voice was warm; she could still remember the long lush languor of that evening, the cold stone at the epicentre of their warm wrapped skin. This surprised Julia. She looked at him. She had never disliked Quentin – it just seemed inevitable ten years ago that she wouldn't stay with him. She was young, things were happening. She wasn't going to be a waitress all her life.

There were three empty bottles of rioja now, pushed to one side on the table. Julia's eyebrows were drooping, but beneath them her eyes kept up a sparkly vigil. She was being flattered and she was enjoying it.

'So don't you see – I don't know where to put you. Where you fit in in my life. You're no category – uncategorizable. Undefinable.' Quentin was addressing the rough surface of the table top, which he was digging at with his thumbnail. The flamenco performers were laughing and talking at the bar. All the other tables were empty. 'You forced me to withdraw from loving you, which I did – I had no choice.' He picked at the table for a while, then looked up. 'It's like – you know – I don't know, there's a splinter and it finally works its way out and it's you, and I want to know what happens to it now.' He looked at the flamenco dancers. 'Do I throw it away or put it in a scrapbook – ' she was admiring the sculpt of his neck when he turned back – 'or drive it back in?' More laughter from the bar. He leaned over the table, head in hands, and didn't speak until she'd looked at everything else and had to look at him. His voice was labored and unjoyous, a hapless traveler reciting directions he can't fathom: 'I loved you. *I loved you.* That was supposed to be it. Everything else was going to take care of itself, because we'd taken care of the only thing that mattered.' Eye to eye now, red-rimmed, crinkly, one wet at the edges. 'And one day it turned out we hadn't. Now how the hell do you – totally unprepared – go about dealing with that? Huh? How do you throw yourself into aborted happily ever afters?'

Something shared, at last: unjoyousness. 'Don't talk about aborting things – '

' – Why did you go?'

'Oh Christ, Quentin, that was ten years ago.' She pulled back but didn't let up looking at him; she'd become hard, she wanted her eyes to sear straight into his skull.

'Why did you? I was ready to do anything.'

She didn't want to hurt him; she'd loved him unlike any other, for a while. 'Which is just what I didn't want. I wanted some give and take – my God, Quentin, some friction. I don't know. Maybe I'm weird. Maybe I distrust feeling happy.'

'And Madhat?'

The flamenco performers were leaving quietly and tiredly, looking around like last-out office workers checking the lights. 'Madhat was all friction. He demanded support, on his own terms. He was about as good for me as you, only in the opposite direction.'

That pendant nestled so fucking cozily. 'And now?'

'Now?'

'You still distrust feeling happy?'

Julia was chewing the inside of her cheek. Her stare had glassed over, dropped. 'I don't know. I have a hard time remembering feeling happy.'

'You seeing anybody now?'

'No. Not really. I don't know anyone – don't have the time.' She considered. 'I don't think I know myself.'

'*I* know you.'

Palpable, clubfooted dread. No response.

'. . . And?' Finally. Which hard management woman had uttered this?

He surprised himself – he didn't say, 'I can help you.' So he had moved on after all. Instead he shrugged his shoulders. 'I don't know. You . . . you once made me feel – complete.

Whole. The greatest feeling I've ever known. I miss it. I need it. I want it back.'

15) *Without your love I am nothing at all.*

'That's all.'

'And your pregnant wife – '

16) And my pregnant wife.

Quentin's pregnant wife was at that moment wiping tears on the sleeve of his robe and pouring out her unfounded suspicions over the phone to her best friend Linda, who was airily quoting from the latest self-help bestseller she was deeply involved with: 'It's a documented fact, pet, that men focus more on images. Like pretty girls, other women, suchlike. Now us women, Dr Dyotson says, we're much more *sophisticated*. We demand the whole package, the support, the commitment. Men can just, pardon my French, screw anybody without feeling anything. And do, all the time. Their support record is appalling, says Dr Dyotson. But women, she says, we're so much *deeper*. We've got so much more to *offer*. There's this one line, it'll tell you so much what you're feeling – I'll get the book, hang on a minute, pet, it's upstairs in bed with Roger – '

The line went dead. The baby in Sue's belly began kicking.

Julia considered.

In Quentin's head uncertainties were routing facts wholesale.

Bruce 'n' Fred 'n' Gettin' Out

You're too old for this tomfoolery, goes the little white angel on my right shoulder. *You've been somebody else most of your adult life and it's time you were yourself for a change.*

Nah, fuck that fairy, goes the smoldering red devil on my left. *You're only as old as the women you feel – and face it, you're never ever gonna feel so many of 'em, so young and so free and so plentiful, anywhere else in the world . . . Besides where you gonna go? New York? LA? London? Rutgers? Don't make me laugh, pal.*

My fingers gently strumming the guitar on the porch in the soft summer rain. Not much beach action today – everybody's already hit the bars or's cruising the malls. Just hanging out, sitting in a rusty deck chair, hoping this flophouse we rented for the summer doesn't collapse on us. Strumming.

Reffing today's Good v. Evil fight.

Evil wins a round and I go get a Genny Cream.

Up until recently, Evil won most rounds. Good just took a licking and kept on ticking. Lately, though, I don't know.

Evil's tiring. I'm tiring. And yet Good still isn't looking too attractive – just seems to be the only untried option.

Bottle hisses, half the contents go down my front, the other half down my throat. Warm. Good clinging to my shoulder like a mountain goat in a monsoon: *Stop it all now. Get out before you're in too deep. Look at Shelby.*

Look at him – been doing the clone band scene practically longer than the originals. Was Jim Morrison for a while in The End, Jerry Garcia in Long Strange Trip and now the Boss in Hazy Davy and the Mission Men. And nobody cares that he's about thirty pounds overweight and balding – hey, so are most of the originals, the ones still alive. No, Shelby's particular genius lies in being able to sound just like the record, so you can close your eyes at the gig and pretend you're back in the comfort of your own home.

You see, says Good, *my point exactly. This whole, ahem, scene, is a dangerous farce.*

Evil leans around my neck. *Tell that to his dick.*

Hazy Davy and the Mission Men are currently the number one Springsteen clone band down the Shore. My outfit Backstreets of Fire are number two. We're better musicians, but we don't look or sound enough like Bruce and The E Streeters. Larry Gulamerian, our Bruce, can rock your jock off, but he's got this damned trained voice – took opera lessons for a couple of years. Tends to lean on the vibrato when he should wail. He also looks more like Shelby than the Boss, which doesn't make anything any easier for either of them.

As for me, personally I think I've got Miami Steve's licks down much better than Marty, Shelby's Miami Steve; but you know, he's got more money, so every time Miami Steve goes and changes his guitar sound Marty can afford to go and change his. I've got this dirty little Ibanez copy – a copy of a copy of a Strat – and some pedals and stuff I play it through, but generally it sounds like what it is. A dirty little Ibanez copy bought for peanuts in Elizabeth. Show me big money and I'll show you a big sound.

So anyway, I'm sitting on the porch thinking, I may go here.

I may go there, I may go any fucking where. Just sitting and strumming my dirty little copy, when a twelfth-hand Toyota rusts up and out jumps our sax player, Richie Bleemberg.

'So this is where you're hiding out,' he goes.

'I got nothing to hide,' I go. 'I'm clean.' He makes his way up the broken front walk and up onto the porch. He makes to sit down on some of our porch furniture.

'Not that one,' I go, 'the bottom falls out.'

'Just like Backstreets of Fire when everybody hears the news,' he goes.

'Hey?'

But Richie's not gonna divulge his hard-earned secrets that easy. 'What-'a'-ya-got, no manners? Ya not gonna even offer me a Genny Cream?'

I'm just about to get another one for myself, so it's not a problem. 'Richie, for you, anything.' I bow, sim-sa-la-bim Carson style, and go inside.

When I come out Richie's got my axe and's trying to play it upside down, on account of he's left-handed. He's not doing bad, but he can only manage bar chords, which bore the shit out of me, so I throw his Genny Cream at him.

He catches it on the fly. 'What, no doily?'

I laugh.

'You'll be laughing out of the other side of your face, you young whippersnapper, when you hear what I've got to say,' he messes around in his old-man voice.

I take a seat, put my feet up on the porch railing, careful to rest them over the part where there are still some supports. Even so, there's a hell of a lot of wobbling. 'OK, I'm comfortable,' I go. 'You may proceed.'

Richie takes an experimental sip of his Genny Cream, like one of those opera singers spraying their mouths before the big aria. He clears his throat a couple of times.

'For fuck's sake, Richie. It's not opening night at the Met. Get on with it.'

'Yeah, all right,' he goes. 'It's just this's *serious*.'

I swallow, listen to the rain drumming quietly, insistently on the porch roof.

And then Richie hits me with it.

'Miami Steve is leaving the E Street Band.'

– And then there's that fucking angel on my right shoulder going, *this shall be a sign unto you* –

'He's not.'

'He is.' Richie leans back in his chair, takes a theatrical big sip. His chair creaks alarmingly, begins to fold up with him in it.

'Sorry,' I go, 'forgot to tell you. That one's busted too.'

Richie gets out just in time. The chair clatters into a heap on the floor. He looks around. 'Anything else I should know?'

'How d'you know he's leaving?'

'Heard it on the MTV news. Lead story.'

See, says the angel, *that's the way it's going around here. You make your living mocking the life of a rock star, you foul his footsteps in his own back yard, and the rest of the world still knows about everything before you. Get out before your life becomes a complete travesty.*

Devil must be out getting some more Genny Creams or something.

'Springsteen name a replacement?'

'Yeah. Nils Lofgren.'

Richie hovering around me, watching for signs of shock, which he gets.

Oh Jesus.

Now I know Nils Lofgren – caught his act a couple years ago at the Stone Pony, and OK, I can put a bandana around my head, one of my mother's clip-on hoop earrings on one ear and jump up and down and in a dark room and I'm sorta Miami Steve, but Nils Lofgren – he's about four foot nothing, shorter than the Boss even, built like a fire hydrant. Has this trampoline thing onstage he bounces around on when things get a little slow.

'Shit.'

'No shit. I mean, so that means now we get you doing Nils

Lofgren doing Miami Steve.' Richie goes into his astronaut voice. 'I think we got a reality problem here, Houston.'

'You're telling me. I'm about a foot and a half taller than him, for starters.'

The screen door slams. Angelina's dress waves. Like a vision, she dances across the porch and goes to sit down.

'Not there,' I go. 'Leg's broken.'

She settles for a bit of porch railing, parks her bottom right on top of it, her dress flowing out into the rain. She waggles her ass a bit, frowns.

I wonder if she's wearing panties.

That'll be the Devil back.

'What's this about Miami Steve?' she goes.

'He's out, gone, history – ' Richie puts on his MTV video jock's voice. 'Left the band to pursue promising solo commitments. We wish him well.'

'We wish he'd given us a little advance notice,' I go. I can hear Larry now, 'I gotta wife, three kids, a mortgage and a boat sinking down Manasquan basin, I need a Nils Lofgren clone!'

'Maybe,' goes Richie, 'maybe you could, like those old vaudeville routines, play on your knees with a pair of shoes sticking out underneath. You know, like that guy who played Toulouse-Lautrec in the movies.'

'He didn't do that in the movies,' goes Angelina. 'He's a real midget. I saw it on *Secrets of the Hollywood Studios*. They nominated him for an Academy Award because they felt sorry for him.'

Now I like Angelina, and in the right light I might even love Angelina, but when she starts talking trash I really wish she'd dump it at sea. 'Look, this is serious. You understand? We got a gig in two days' time, and if I don't figure out what to do, Backstreets of Fire're gonna be playing with a big hole where their guitarist used to be.'

So they give me a couple of minutes of silence, but I can't come up with anything, other than this image of myself with my guitar slung over my shoulder riding freight trains to

California, howling at the prairie moon with a tenth of Mad Dog sticking out my back pocket . . .

. . . And I get this feeling Good and Evil have struck some kind of deal behind my back.

'Look,' goes Richie finally, 'I gotta go. *General Hospital* be on in a few minutes.'

Angelina shrieks and jumps up.

World's full of bugs, and they get just about anywhere. Serves her right for not wearing panties.

But it's not that at all. 'Oh-my-god you're right!' and she's disappeared inside, dress damply trailing after her like an old sheet somebody's used to wash the car.

I look at Richie. 'Do you get like that about soap operas?'

' 'Course not. I just watch 'em to get my role models straight – just in case I decide to give up this mad carefree existence and settle down to being a brain surgeon.'

He went to Rutgers for a while, I think.

'You gonna be at The Traffic Circle tonight?' he calls from the car.

'I dunno. Suppose so.' This is Hazy Davy's big night, and the whole Shore's bound to be there.

'Well, if you are, I'll be down the OB Diner before. Lining my stomach.'

'Whatever.'

'Well, Mr Gulamerian,' he goes in his brain surgeon's voice, 'we can give you a replacement guitarist, but the chances of survival are about one in thirty-three and a third. And even if the operation is successful there's no guarantee the new guitarist won't be rejected by the other organs. And drums. And bass. And vocals. And public.'

Each of those shouted out the window as he rattles away.

Rutgers.

I mean Jesus.

So here I am down the Traffic Circle parking lot, one hand parked on Angelina's very fine ass, the other flicking a cigarette into the night. Place's filling up pretty quickly, like it used to in the old days when the Boss came down fairly regular, when he was still nervous of fame and touched base with us a lot. Nowadays, I dunno, I guess he's come to terms with it and comes down to remind himself why he wanted out in the first place. Did that the other night – dropped in right here in the middle of Hazy Davy's set, jumped onstage, did a couple of numbers, and next morning all you heard was *He* was at the Traffic Circle last night and everybody carrying on like the Second Coming's just happened on the corner of Fourth and Ocean. And of course, Shelby becomes an instant megastar – even got a little spot on the MTV news. You know, thirty seconds of Shelby saying what an average Joe Bruce is, how he and Bruce go way back, how the Mission Men'll be down the Traffic Circle again Saturday night and you never know . . .

And so you got a parking lot full of all these North Jersey kids, a sprinkling of New York and Pennsylvania plates, even one or two from Connecticut and Christ, *Indiana* – obviously it's Showtime down the Shore in a big way. So I figure we better hustle ourselves in there like now, so I reach into the car, pull out my axe, and steer Angelina towards the fire exit.

And I can't believe what I'm seeing. They got a bouncer on the fire exit. How else an honest hardworking musician supposed to get into the place gratis? But it's OK, it's Big Louie from the garage, and he's gonna have to let us in because he fucked up my replacement tailpipe.

Maybe a small town isn't so bad.

All this getting me so twisted I can't even tell who said that, Good or Evil.

'Hey, Louie.'

'Hey, Mike. Hey, Angelina.'

'Hey, Louie.'

'So why you back here? They decide you too mean to go out front?'

Louie likes the thought of that. 'Nah. It's just Bruno's scared they gonna get so many people, they gonna start bashing down all the windows and doors to get in like.'

'Sounds serious.'

'Lissen. I did security over Convention Hall for Jefferson Starship in '75, and that's *nothin'* compared to this. Ya know what I'm sayin'?'

Better him than me. 'Yeah.'

'And the other thing – get this.' He points at the sagging battered fire door. 'That's now the music business entrance.'

Amazement.

'Bruno goes to me, he goes – the music business gonna be here tonight, Louie. I'm gonna give 'em passes and send 'em around to you at the music business entrance. And I'm going, like, what? And Bruno goes again, the music business. Like it was the Mob or something.'

'Well, you know I saw on *Dark Secrets of the Glamor Stars* where they said the Mob runs the music business and that Lionel Ritchie is their contact and if he wants somebody killed all he has to do is pick up the phone and they'll do it.'

Like I say, I could almost love Angelina but she has this habit of blowing it.

'Well listen,' I go, 'we're the music business, so why don't we try out the entrance?' And start hustling Angelina towards the door.

But Louie, I think all this talk about the music business and the Mob's got to him. 'Hang on a minute,' and he blocks the doorway with one big sweaty arm.

And I'm, like, gimme a break Louie, I known you ten years, you fucked up my tailpipe, I'm not Carlo Gambino, let's just get on with real life, hey? But I don't say any of this because I can see in his eyes he's a little wired and out on Planet Powercrazed to boot, so I just stop and say, 'What's the problem?'

'The problem is,' Louie goes, 'is I don't see no pass.'

Small-town, small-time nickel and dime. I hear the train a-comin', a-comin' down the tracks – sampled with California here I come. 'Louie, I talked to Shelby this afternoon. He said tonight's not gonna be any different.'

'Shelby ain't payin' my salary.'

'Look Louie – ' do I have to do this? – 'you remember last month I came in with that rusted-out exhaust system dragging its ass so bad you were afraid the sparks on your forecourt were gonna blow us all to kingdom come?'

And, you know, shortly thereafter we're knocking on the dressing room door.

Shelby himself answers, and I swear to God he's got *mascara* on. Very hazy indeed. His eyes wild and jumpy, and I realize for once it's not speed, it's genuine fear.

'Oh,' he goes.

'Thanks Shelby. Dee-light-ful to see you too.' Angelina can turn a phrase, when she wants to. I like that about her.

We go in.

'Yo, Mike!' Royce calls from the other side of the room. He's Hazy Davy's sax man, about forty, and a great guy. He's also black, like The Big Man in the E Street Band. This is another reason why Hazy Davy is number one. Our sax man Richie looks like Woody Allen stretched out on a rack.

I give him a high five. 'Yo, Royce.'

'Big day, man, big day. We got four of 'em in the crowd tonight. Like ducks in a shootin' gallery. Gonna pick 'em off – ' he points his sax like a 12-bore – 'BANG! there goes Columbia! BANG! there goes Warner Brothers! BANG! there goes Geffen! BANG! there goes . . .' he lowers his sax. 'Who're them fourth cats anyway?'

'Look, will you shut-the-fuck up?' yells Shelby. He's sitting over in the corner, scribbling on a piece of paper, frowning.

'What's with Little Jack Horner?' goes Angelina.

'Ah, don't worry about him. He just thought you somebody important.' Royce's got this deep chuckle, like Darth Vader giggling. 'I presume y'all heard 'bout our special guest star the other night?'

'He wanted to know why we weren't doing any of his new stuff,' goes Shelby. 'You know, all that acoustic boring shit. So I says, Brucie man, nobody likes it. Around here, I says, old habits die hard. Everybody still goes for

153

the old stuff. The Jersey stuff. The roots music, man, I says.'

'What'd he say?'

'He said–' butts in Vin Principato, Hazy Davy's bass player whose brother used to play with Southside Johnny before he got famous, 'thanks for the gig and we'll have to do it again sometime.'

'Yeah, but he didn't say it like that Vinnie.'

'What're ya talkin', he didn't say it like that? Those're his exact words!'

'Yeah, but Vinnie, he was a lot more enthusiastic,' goes Shelby.

'Tuh hell you say,' goes Vinnie.

'He was,' goes Shelby to us, like we're court judges and he's trying to get off for DWI.

'And then them A & R men start callin',' goes Royce, yanking his feather cleaner thing through his horn. 'Columbia, Epic, Geffen and them other cats.'

'Virgin,' goes Vin.

'Now there's a label for me,' goes Royce. 'With all due respect,' and he does a little bow with the feather cleaner in Angelina's direction.

'Shit,' I go. I don't care who knows it, I'm impressed. That's some company to be in.

'Ain't shit baby,' goes Royce. 'That the sweet smell of success.'

'Yeah, his, not ours. So let's not get all fuckin' bigheaded about it, OK?' Vin's a bit, I think, on edge, plus I know there's this big rivalry thing between him and his brother, who got married and got a day job just before Southside Johnny made it, and who's going around town lately laying odds that Vin does exactly the same thing now with Jo Anne. Lotta bitterness there, and you know, the Italians love one of their own who goes out and makes it against the odds. Perry Como springs to mind, and Sinatra, and that guy who sang 'Volare'. That sorta thing.

So there's this enormous silence like Raceway Park the

second before they wave the checkered flag. I nudge Angelina to try to get her to say something funny, but all she says is 'Ow' and nobody laughs.

Finally Royce pulls out a tenth of Mad Dog and passes it around and that seems to do the job.

'Well,' Angelina goes, 'I suppose we better get going if we wanna be able to tell our grandchildren we were there,' and this time just about everybody laughs. Except Shelby and Vin, who are not liking each other very much at this moment in time.

'Yeah, OK,' goes Shelby, and he follows us to the door. Angelina is through it and I am almost, too, when Shelby grabs me by the shoulder.

'Listen, Mike, man – whahabout this Miami Steve shit? What're you and Backstreets gonna do?'

I shrug. 'Dunno. Haven't talked to them yet. Maybe take a vacation. What're you guys gonna do about Marty?'

'Dunno. He's somewhere backstage fuckin' sulking about it now. You'd think he lost his only goddamn friend.' But the real reason he's pulled me aside is he wants to talk about the future. The post-signing future. He's flying right now, out on one of Saturn's rings on fear and excitement and adrenalin, and I'm envious. That feeling is just about the greatest you can have with your clothes on. Musicians live for those few trembly minutes before a big gig, that couple of seconds when everybody's screaming for you and you can absolutely do no wrong.

So I am envious. I'd ditch all thoughts of getting out, I'd personally drop-kick Good off the end of the Conventional Hall pier, if I could be in Shelby's position right now.

Which is why, when he asks me to I want to be a Mission Man, I damn near drop my axe case on his foot.

'Look,' he goes, 'let's look at the facts. Bruce is great, he's the Boss, we're all agreed, but he's past his prime. His best record was almost ten years ago. His new one, it's OK – '

– Heresy! my angel should be crying, but I get the feeling he's listening very closely instead –

'But it's no "Born to Run". See? Now when Hazy Davy gets out there we're not just gonna be just another clone band with a contract. No way José. We're gonna *move*. I got plans.'

'Go on.'

Shelby takes a breath, starts talking very quickly. I can't keep track, he's so excited – fuck this tribute-band shit, change Hazy Davy's name and style, go where the money is – heavy metal. Today's rock 'n' roll. To do that right needs another guitarist, more firepower. He pats my axe case. Much more firepower. Then bust out in a big way – nationally. Get the hell outa this dump. When tonight's done he wants me to come around his place and talk some more.

Good and Evil have definitely done this deal.

'If you get a contract, what're you gonna be called?'

He looks at me like Charles Manson or something. '*When* we get a contract we'll be called – Leopardskin Whiplash.'

Not even Evil's got the heart to ask what the costumes'll be like.

Gillian Smythe had chosen the short straw and as punishment got sent to Jersey. Rather like being sent to Coventry, only closer. Or maybe the whole thing had been fixed from the start, simply because she was new in the research department. Anyway, here she was on this gargantuan Garden State Parkway – made the M25 seem like a country lane – peering through the windscreen wipers, choking in the heat and smog. Why didn't the rain, the bloody rain around which everything back in England revolved, have any effect in this bloody place? It's supposed to cool everything down, green everything up, freshen the place . . . Not here. She hurled a quarter at the tollbooth. It missed. Swearing, she threw open the car door. A blast of hot humid air hit her full on the face. Pissing, stinking rain. Behind her, car horns began to honk. No sign of the errant quarter – she'd have to get down on her sunburned knees and hunt for it.

Bollocks.

Oh Gilly, we just love your accent, they'd told her when they'd come to London to recruit. Gilly (that vulgar Yank hard 'G', like she was something glassy-eyed on the fishmonger's slab) they promised blithely, with an accent like that you'll be on the air in no time. Start with a little research job just to get the hang of things, then Bang! You know, we Americans just can't get enough of your English accents. We could sit right here all day and listen to you read the phone book. You're just what we want.

Go, all her girlfriends said at the time, are you loopy? It's *America*! New York City! You'll be making so much money you won't know what to do with it! You'll mix with all the Beautiful People! You'll be able to get hamburgers at four in the morning!

Gillian groaned. It was a career move. She went.

The Beautiful People, she knew from experience, weren't. They lived on ugly things her father imported for them – bland mustard, hideous floral-print patio furniture (for patios that didn't exist), cartons of cartoon breakfast cereals, running shoes for a spongy psychedelic sort of running which left tracks in the English mud like the first steps on the moon. 'Wha'-da-ya mean I cain't get no Genny Creams over here' was her father's call to arms – a signal from the US military command to mount a painstaking campaign involving locating the item in question Stateside, tracking it down, securing it, transferring it to base at Aldershot, and finally submitting it to routine examination by a select panel of top brass and local dignitaries (in Operation Genny Cream, a particularly lengthy and detailed examination, convened with burgers and franks in the Smythe barbecue pit). Only then was it presented to the grateful personnel of the Aldershot base. The natives, at first inevitably shy and reserved, never let their Britishness get the better of them – first empty Genny Cream bottles would disappear from the army rubbish bins only to reappear in pride of place in the local pub collection, then odd Genny Creams would be discovered for sale at a ridiculous price in the off-licence. Finally Mr Smythe would be forced into supplying all of Aldershot, then neighboring towns, and so on. Nice little earner, was his verdict, with attendant purveying of goodwill and performing of civic duty a PR bonus.

But purveying of goodwill was really Mrs Smythe's department. A steady stream of Yanks lumbered around the coffee mornings and cocktail parties of Gillian's youth, mutating her mother into some mid-Atlantic mishap cut adrift from both sides. Her voice remained a constant pantomime of there always being an Engalnd: 'Oh, Duane, deah, I shan't be able to control myself, not even one weensy bit, if I have another of your Slow Comfortable Screws, deah', yet her body positively exulted in Lee Riders, old US college sweatshirts and any other authentic hand-me-downs she could snatch up at the army wives' jumble sales.

For Gillian this dichotomy was hell. On the playground she found herself in demand by both sides for Froot Loops, Tonka Toys and super balls, often resulting in her running home in tears. To escape, she often decamped to the branches of a holm oak out on the army artillery range, where, to the rumble and crash of the Yanks bombing hell out of Britain, she read Tintin comics and desperately wished she were French.

She could just see the quarter, about halfway under the car. Which would mean hot humiliating slithering on her belly, a belly which the American sun had treated most inhospitably. Air conditioning. She needed air conditioning. She gasped like a fish out of water. This bloody, bloody, *bloody* climate! How was she supposed to –

Knees crackling, she drew herself up to her full five foot one.

Sod it.

She hurled herself into her car and roared off. The tollbooth bell rang in her ears like the air after target practice.

She'd been in New York almost two years, doing the most piddling and pathetic research work. Her career move, it seemed, consisted mostly of researching instant coffee brand satisfaction among TV producers. The money was OK, but once she'd counted the cost of living in Manhattan (both in dollars and sheer bloody aggro), plus not one but *three* income taxes, her jumped-up bedsit in Islington and her pleasant (if slightly dozy) research job in London suddenly looked a lot better.

Don't worry, her girlfriends told her over the phone. Women in business get a much better deal in the States, they're ten years ahead of us in sexual equality on the job. And all that rubbish in the papers about getting a place in London now because in a few years England will be the place to be, what with 1992 and the European Community and all that, is just that – rubbish. OK, so there may already be some of these weird new Euro-jobs around, and so it does look like we are going to build that channel tunnel with the French after all, and so maybe because of *that* things *are* starting to hot up, but you wouldn't believe what it's doing to the traffic. Oh dear. Simply awful. You can hardly get the new Golf into work these days. Some of her friends had even been forced to link up the office IBM to the home one and work from there, just to get something done. No, she was much better where she was. All her European friends were simply *vert* with envy.

Gillian was driving very fast, probably not as fast as a new Golf, but certainly close to the limit of a rental Chevy. Like going down to Brighton to interview old age pensioners this job was – stake out, in the words of her boss, this Traffic Circle joint and see if Springsteen's around. If he is, get Gregg to film everything he can point the camera at. If not, see if there's any kind of a Jersey Shore angle worth doing. If *that* doesn't work, hell with it, shoot some seagulls and we'll go with wildlife. Just come back with something to fill that last five minutes, got me Gilly baby? And make sure it's not just a load of seagulls humping, hey? We run a family show here.

Her mother would've loved him.

Gillian found this thought so diverting she rocketed clear past the Asbury Park exit. And spent the rest of the day touring South Jersey, fuming in air-conditioned comfort. Near someplace contentiously named Pleasantville the rain gave way to equally stifling sun and she noticed the landscape for the first time – all flat and gritty, hummocked here and there with gnarled, sandblasted trees. Spookily like the Aldershot artillery range, all those innocent oaks and alders and birches caught in the NATO firing lines. Gillian felt a sudden sadness. Which only made her madder. She redoubled her efforts to find Asbury Park.

When she finally squealed to a halt in the Traffic Circle lot there was no sign of Gregg or the mobile unit. Maybe they were here somewhere – the place was chock-a-block with cars. And kids. Everywhere she looked she saw kids – embroidered and bedenimed bodies, a sprawling uniformed Levi's army sweating war against the climate.

The climate. They could keep the climate. God, she wanted a bath.

Yet there was something going on here. She could feel it in her researcher's bones – a buzz. An Event. Something much more than just five minutes at the end of a lifestyle program. Gillian looked around, chewed on her lip. After two years of sodding slogging, this could finally be a break! Now where the hell were Gregg and the crew? She could ad-lib a quick to-camera piece leaned up against one of those pick-up trucks, then a quick nip inside for Springsteen, maybe even a quote or two . . . Suddenly the air around her was cool, the breeze off the ocean fresh. In the gathering dark shapes were detaching themselves from cars and loping towards the Traffic Circle entrance. Gillian followed briskly, her peeling pinkness rosy.

Inside all activity was blocked by a tentacled, money-waving monster to one side of the stage. The bar. Gillian frowned and got as comfortable as she could against a sticky black pillar, half-scanning the crowd for Gregg, half-scripting her piece.

As she did, the monster vomited up a tall pigeon-chested

young man with a complexion like topography. He came to rest next to Gillian, and without any introduction commenced talking about himself.

'I have an impeccable sense of balance.' He pointed at the urine-colored drink in his hand. 'Otherwise I'd be wearing this instead of drinking it. I've had years of practice. I only come here for the beer.'

Gillian looked away, continued scanning.

'Sooooooo,' he said. It sounded like the scream of a man thrown from an airplane. He leaned up against Gillian's pillar, just about but not quite touching her, his right leg tucked up underneath him.

He looks like a stork, the corner of Gillian's eye informed her, a starving stork with a faceful of volcanic activity. Why do Americans always assume you want to know their life stories? She turned her attention to the entrance.

'You here to verify the sighting?'

She meant to sweep over him on her way back across the room, but he spoke just as her glance hit him. It froze.

'Pardon?'

'The sighting. The second coming – or is it the third?'

Gillian frowned.

'You know – Him. The Alpha and Omega. The Boss. The Son of Man, out now on LP and cassette.'

'If you mean Bruce Springsteen, in fact I am.' Delivered in the same tone her mother sometimes employed at her parties to remind rambunctious Yanks of the sanctity of the English home.

'Well then, you came to the right place, honey.' And this one paid about as much attention. He made an expansive gesture with his arms. 'Behold the faithful, the Denim Disciples of the Demigod.' He stopped abruptly, made a noise, took out a notebook, scribbled.

Seeing her opportunity Gillian attempted an exit, but the crowd had pinned her against the pillar. She was stuck, without her crew, without an escape, with both the house lights and her breakthrough shot fading fast.

'Pretty good, hey?' blurted the Stork suddenly. 'About the denim disciples. The alliteration. Goldblatt always comes down on me about the alliteration. These days I put it in just to piss him off.' He adopted a vapid grin, one much favored in a current credit card ad. 'Hi. Do you know me? I'm a famous music journalist with the *Jersey Rockline*, that well-known freebie music paper, available at all discerning jukejoints and greasy spoons for the princely sum of not one red cent. Cheap at half the price.' His ostrich neck with its bulbous Adam's apple tilted dangerously towards her. 'You're English aren't you?'

Fading. Trapped. 'Mm-hmm.'

'Well, lucky you. Here, you guys invented the language. Cop a load of this.' He cleared his throat, stopped. 'I mean, give this your attention.' He started reading from his notebook in a voice easily pitched above the crowd. 'In time-honored tradition it's convention time here at Asbury Park. Delegates from every imaginable stage of Springsteen discipleship are crowding the floor, from the denim deadbeats of His – with a capital H – His early days to the pec-flexing, bolo-tied mythmongers of the latest incarnation, all eager to help in the rolling away of the stone at The Traffic Circle tonight – ' He gasped a breath, fixed her in his droopy eyes. 'You get that double imagery? It's a bit complex, but I keep telling Goldblatt, people've got brains, even rock fans, they like to take them out and use them once in a while.'

Gillian was about to use that line to finish him off, but he seemed to anticipate it and slipped past her: 'Girls in jeans, girls in wavy dresses, barefoot girls drinking warm beer on the hood of a Dodge as the mood stipulates – those're all lines from his songs, see, I've worked them in – stipulates, drift in and out or simply hang around, searching for velvet ribs to wrap their arms around. You know "Born to Run"?'

She did, of course. And wished she didn't. All those appalling army base discos . . . She told him so in no uncertain terms.

'Oh. Well here, how about this – *down the Shore*, as it's quaintly monikered by locals and tourists alike, the Boss is the Business – just about the only one in an area being rapidly eroded by disinterest and dereliction – more alliteration, I love it, I absolutely love it, don't *you* love it – even as the oily ocean batters the beach. An area spared by one rock*meister*'s vision of the romance in its ruin – and now the Shore, shored up, pumps that vision for all it's worth.' He was hitting his stride. 'And what of the faithful, the clone-band *canaille*? As undemanding as the bands themselves. All geezers – there, that's a good English word for you – who expect second best and accept third readily, first having high-tailed it out long ago under their own noses. As Nietzsche said, the reverence due to every tradition increases from generation to generation. The tradition finally becomes holy and inspires awe. Our local leftovers might not be the real holy men, might not have even touched the hem of their garments, but they're that one generation closer than their congregation, which inspires tonight's awe. So praise the Lord and pass the pastiche. Ayyyyy-men.' He clutched his spiral Bible to his concave chest.

There was a pause during which she didn't suck in her breath admiringly, so he did it for her. 'Pretty damn political, hey? We need more muckraking, I keep telling Goldblatt, a frank dialogue between the rock fan and the music press, but all he wants is frigging advertising. You know? Advertising is king.'

Gregg must be around the back, that was it, setting up in front of the artists' entrance. The straw Gillian was clutching at slipped further through her grasp. If there was an artists' entrance in this tip. By now her researcher's sense had told her tonight there wasn't going to be much in the way of art. Particularly if this prize pillock here was anything to go by. Where the hell was Springsteen? Where was the *culture* in this goddamn country? 'Excuse me,' she said, seeing a sudden available gap in the crowd. She disappeared into it.

'English music sucks!' he shouted after her, alliteration failing him.

*

And of course, the gig's a major-league abortion. Angelina wants to go when everybody else does, when there's nothing left to throw at them, but I don't know, I guess I feel some kind of masochistic loyalty to the living hell they're going through.

One thing at least's been decided because of that night – I ain't never gonna be no Leopardskin Whiplasher or Mission Man for sure. Miracle Man's more like what Shelby's gonna need now. Along with a new sax and bass player.

And I need to stop listening to those two cartoon monkeys on my back and make a decision.

What was it that guy in the *Rockline* said, hang on, it's here in the garbage, he said, ah – 'For some reason best known to themselves the band decided to play all their own numbers, perhaps in the hopes of putting the fear of God into the Son of Man should he happen to appear, which he didn't. Lucky him, because their songs were lumbering jumbles of cliché one step over and several down from anything distantly listenable. The lead singer's voice slipped and slid like the clutch of a '64 Buick Skylark all over the stage, transforming intended anthemic first-punchers into soupy soup-cons – ' whatever they are – 'of sound. The guitarist and one-time Miami Steve performed most of the gig either with his back to the faithful or in the wings, his Last Post in memory of his departed hero a feedbacked ululation of unbecomingness. This all caused the multitude much distress, and sensing false prophets, they reacted first with a stoning of beer cups then a mass exodus, seeking the promised land over at the Chatterbox or Jimmy Byrne's. As – ' some German guy I can't pronounce – 'said, "If ye would go up high, then use your own legs!" '

He's right, I think, the *Rockline* guy, but why can't he write in English?

Plus the '64 Skylark was an automatic.

So Springsteen doesn't show, the A & R guys walk out holding their ears after about the fourth number, and so does that TV crew that came down, and by the time Bruno finally takes pity on Hazy Davy and cuts the power there's only me and Angelina and the bartender. Shelby's up there clinging on to the mike stand like it's a life raft and he's capsized, everybody else in a daze crackling around on this carpet of beer cups. And Bruno goes up to Shelby, and Shelby's watching him, and Bruno holds the envelope with Hazy Davy's money up over his head high as he can go, and lets go of it, and it just flutters on to the stage. Like a newspaper in the wind.

And Shelby's watching it, haunted.

And for a second there I think I'm gonna lose it.

And Shelby just watches it fall, and then goes, 'What happened?'

And Bruno goes, 'You bombed's what happened. Put the Springsteen stuff back in and *maybe* I'll see you next week.'

And Shelby slides down the length of the mike stand into a crackly heap.

And I think it really is time to go.

Geraniums, spat Gillian at the TV, bloody geraniums. Pipped at the post by sodding flowers. The screen was then filled with a very large black woman in a Garden State Parkway uniform, who explained earnestly and self-consciously that the geraniums on the Alfred E. Driscoll Memorial Bridge weren't blooming this year as well as last, and she thought it was asbestos in the air from Johns-Manville. Then there was another shot from the roof of the mobile unit of planters full of stunted geraniums, the camera pulling back to reveal an enormous traffic jam stretched over the bridge as far as the eye could see. Then it was back to the studio for smug, smiling Bryce Bumrick ('Bryce Bumcrack!' she shouted at the TV) who made some typically simpering remark about how they still look better than the geraniums in his back yard, and thanks for watching, the show was over. And there was nothing within reach to throw at the TV.

So this is how it all ends – not with a bang, but a geranium. When she'd finally located Gregg and the crew, Gregg as usual said no worries, because on the way down they'd been stuck in this monster traffic jam, and he'd actually been able to use it to get some good footage, more than enough, in fact, to cover their asses. Some interviews even. Big bubbles no troubles, he cooed in that despicable way which screamed, look at me, aren't I a consummate professional?

Gillian could feel her own reservoir rapidly drying up. Great Gregg, great, she'd painfully grinned before storming off to her car to have a good scream. But upon locating the Chevy she'd discovered the fly window smashed and a hole in the steering column where something undoubtedly essential should have been. Alternator, Gregg said after she'd capped her evening by begging him please to come and look, weird thing to steal. Still down here in the boonies –

What does that mean? muttered Gillian.

Means you're coming home with us, sweetie, Gregg cooed.

Not like this back in Jollie Olde, hey Gilly? he'd chortled later as he bowed and held the post production door open for her.

That 'G' sound again, as in 'get stuffed.'

And get out. Gillian switched off the TV viciously. It was late. She'd had it. There had to be better things to do than take a back seat to Gregg's geraniums. And that . . . *place* they'd sent her to last night, every nightmare barracks disco she'd ever been dragged to . . . This was all wrong. She had to get out. While she was young, because – the phone rang.

It was London calling. Her friends more than a bit tipsy, all huddled around the celphone in Jean-Philippe's Audi. Little partyette, they said giggling, *eine poco célébration* for a deal somebody'd just struck with Jean-Philippe and Salvatore's firm. Like the bleeding United Nations it was here tonight, nobody knew what anybody else was saying, but they were all committed to draining the EEC wine lake all right . . . What was going on over in New York?

'Nothing,' said Gillian.

The next second there was even less.

A few days later I'm between gigs at the Royal Manor North and I see Royce in a diner on Route 1.

'Yo, homeboy,' he goes, grinning.

'Royce, my man.' He's got his axe with him and a look on his face like he's just won Pick Six. 'Whatdja, just get the call from James Brown or something?'

Just grinning, trembling even a bit. 'Bigger.'

Now you don't get a lot bigger than James Brown. 'Let me guess. Virgin's reconsidering Hazy Davy.'

His explosive snort going, don't even talk to me. Whatever he's got up his sleeve, it's major league.

'OK, so I give up. Cut me in. Deal.'

Him grinning so wide he's beginning to look like Satchmo for Chrissake. But with fewer teeth. 'You remember La Bamba?'

'Course I remember La Bamba. Played the bone. Went big with Southside Johnny. Haven't seen him in years.'

Royce nods. 'Me neither. Well dig, day after we went belly-up at The Traffic Circle I get this phone call. And it's La Bamba. And he's like, Royce man, how's it goin', long time, remember the days we used to play all night long, and all that shit. So we shoot the shit for a while and I'm thinkin', man it's my bowling night with my brother-in-law, and La Bamba goes, Royce man I want you come up the city for a little jam. And I'm like what, man? And then La Bamba comes straight – this chick, no make that this *lady*, this *lady* heard about him playin' with Southside and's about to go on some motherfucker of a worldwide tour and's lookin' for a little bit of a horn section, and does he want, and of course he does, so he goes around blows a while and he's in, and cat organizing the horns goes, you know any good sax men?'

'And he goes yeah, of course, Royce Williams, the poor man's Clarence Clemons.'

'Yeah, well sorta, Mike, sorta. See I'm a sorta stand-in. Regular cat got a bit too strung out, ya hear me? So La Bamba says come on down, and I come on down this afternoon, and dude organizing, he hears me blow with the other cats and we're tight and clean and sharp and he goes, you're in.'

Royce blows on his coffee like it was a mouthpiece. 'Just like that.'

'Who's the lady?'

'The Boss.'

'But The Boss is a – '

'Mike, man, you gotta get your head outta that boardwalk life, hear what I'm sayin'? The *other* Boss.'

I'm drawing a big blank. A real big blank. Royce sees it and shakes his head.

'Diana Ross, man. Diana The Boss Ross. She's called it too. Leastways for this tour she gonna be.'

'You're playing sax for *Diana Ross?*'

Royce dunks a big brown donut in his coffee. 'I'm in the horn section, homeboy. Let's put it that way.'

I can't speak. How do these guys *do* it?

He looks at me sort of out the corner of his eye, swallows his mouthful of donut, claps his hands around the back of my neck. 'No more playin' the fantasy nigger for the board-walk scene, man. I'm my own man now.' His nails chipped and rough. 'For me this boardwalk life's through, baby. You oughta quit this scene too. Sound familiar, Mike? . . . That's right. Stop pretending and do something 'fore it's too late.'

'Yeah, of course Royce. I'm getting my shit together.'

'Great.' He goes back to his donut. 'What you doing?'

'Ah – probably going cross-country. Yeah. Out to California. Check out the scene there.'

Royce nods. 'We'll be in LA sometime round about October. Look me up. I'll try and get you some tickets. Who knows – ' he lets loose with one of those Darth Vader chuckles – 'maybe round then Diana's guitarist have a *freak accident*.' He claps me on the neck again. My spine shakes.

And I have to get out of there quick before I lose it again.

And a couple of days later and it's one of those days you get in late August that reminds you September and fall're just around the corner, which always depresses me. So I'm

walking down the boardwalk thinking about things, everything that's gone down, and these two chicks come up to me.
Really foxy-looking, although they couldn't have been more
than about seventeen. And suddenly I'm thinking, hello Betty
maybe I'll hang around for just a minute and one of them
goes, 'Sign our petition.' And I go what? and she explains
that they're circulating this petition to make 'Born to Run'
the Official State Anthem. And I sort of roll my eyes and the
other one, the blonde, she goes 'What?' And I feel suddenly
old, and start telling them how they tried this one already
about five years ago and it didn't quite make it then, and they
both interrupt me and go how this time it's different and
anyway it's such a really, really brilliant song, and all that.

And I go, 'Ladies, it's a song about getting the hell out of
New Jersey.'

And right about this time, where normally good old Good
and Evil'd kick in, nothing happens. *Nada.*

And they go to say something, then don't, then one of
them looks right at me, kinda shy the way that makes me
fall apart inside, and goes, 'Hey, aren't you Miami Steve in
Backstreets of Fire?'

And I go, 'Yeah.'

And all of a sudden they forget all about their petition and
start grabbing me and hauling me over to a bench. And these
two foxy chicks are all over me asking all about the Boss, the
E Street Band, what's gonna happen with Miami Steve and
Nils, did I ever meet them, what were they like . . .

And I'm about to say which Boss, but then I don't know,
maybe there's a little bit of sun suddenly shines down right
on the three of us and it's warm and there's nothing else really
going down, and I don't have all the answers so maybe I just
lie a tiny bit, engage in a *little* deception –

And those two foxy chicks, they just love it. They just
eat it up.

It was very strange, thought Gillian as she walked down the
long corridor to her producer's office, as soon as she'd hung

up the phone last night this debate over whether or not to go ahead and do it seemed to pop into her head fully formed. On the one side somebody – she was almost sure it wasn't her – was saying, yes go ahead, this is an essential move not only for your career but for your emotional growth and well-being, and on the other somebody else was saying, listen, bollocks to that, tell them all to get stuffed and to hell with them.

And she hadn't been able to get rid of either of them. Yet even as she listened to their endless bickering she felt calm, assured, and completely confident in what she was doing. She placed her hand lightly on her producer's door, and ignoring the Holiday Inn Occupied sign slapped over the knob, pushed it open.

He was there directly before her, seeing only interruption and lack of coffee. His ice-blue contact lenses glinted. He spoke slowly and measuredly.

'You're supposed to knock. Everyone knocks. Go back and do it again.'

'Get stuffed.' Quietly.

'What?' The word spiralling upward, like that giddy feeling in the stomach as the elevator climbs.

'Get stuffed,' she repeated, a little louder. 'To hell with you and your job. Get – stuffed.' She almost said it sweetly.

He took a step back, then roared. How dare she, after all he'd, who the hell did she think, she'll never make it in TV he'll make sure of that, and don't think he couldn't, he could, he'd make sure she's blackballed from here to Television City and back again, one goddamn thing he didn't need was some fucking little Limey pissant telling him to get fucked –

'Stuffed,' said Gillian. 'I said stuffed. I don't say fuck.'

She had an attitude problem, did she know that? A big fat attitude problem. And where in hell did she think she was gonna get work with a big fat attitude problem?

'What attitude problem?' said Gillian. 'I'm a European. You're the one with the problem.'

Namely, he discovered, how to shut his gaping office door without his blabbermouth of a secretary seeing.

The Axolotl Grin
of a Champion

'It's cold,' she shouts up to you in the bleachers. She scoops up a handful of water and flings it. It hits. You recoil in fake horror, she in a gigantic grin. You pantomime the witch in *The Wizard of Oz* melting into a free-form puddle. 'Oh Toto,' she calls, 'at last we can go home to Kansas.' Then she remembers the others in the pool. Embarrassed yet still grinning, she retreats into the water.

You've known her since school days, when you were gunning for good grades and she was running with what your parents disdainfully called a fast crowd. You were entranced by her then, her inaccessibility, her precocity, her sex. Just the sight of her unleashed an overload of adolescent crossed signals, a power surge in an already sparking junction box. She attended classes infrequently – really only to ward off expulsion – but in those classes she was a window to a world your parents warned was her just deserts, but which seemed to you a full-course feast, particularly when you considered her solid B+ average. In short, she had it all.

If you could have talked to her you would have begged her to take you along – to the downtown bars (where at fourteen she packed the *présence* of someone far older), to the rampaging all-nighters on the outskirts of town, to the city's countless rock 'n' roll outrages ('Yeah, I saw his cock,' you remember overhearing her shrug to several goggle-eyed friends. 'He was really wasted in the middle of some song and he comes down to the audience and says, do we want to see it, and of course I said yes'). But you couldn't talk to her, not then, nor later when you were at college downtown and occasionally pointed her out – short leather mini, kitten heels, too-tight T-shirt and beat-up leather jacket that proclaimed, Sex And Drugs and Rock And Roll – to incredulous friends. It wasn't until much later, years later, when you bumped into her far from the distraction of the city, in a country town where you'd gone to concentrate on your thesis and she'd gone to dry out, break down, break out, get caught, O.D. and give up.

She has clocked everybody around her – the two old ladies kibitzing in the shallow end, the lone man laboring at lengths, the lifeguard at the far end idly twirling his whistle. She imagines they are all staring at her, particularly the lifeguard, who is lean and well muscled. This makes her aware: her faded track marks are exposed, throbbing; her big thirty-three-year-old's body is suddenly swelling, gargantuan, her snug Speedo a threadbare corset from which she threatens to burst. Her hands flit nervously around her side, ready to catch exploding flesh. For a second your birthday wish to see her swim again is dwarfed by ballooning self-consciousness. She risks an imploring look but you've anticipated it and dived behind the book you've brought. She looks away, takes a slow, deep breath, sinks under the water.

She hasn't been swimming for a long time, really since she was a girl. At least fifteen years since she last swam competitively, twenty since her coach decided she was Olympic material. Her own thirteen-year-old's decision that she was not she's never completely explained, but you're convinced that that decision led to the one a year later never to compete in anything with a future attached. ('Your parents must have been heartbroken when you gave up swimming,' you'd surmised. 'My parents,' she'd answered drily, 'couldn't give a flying fuck.')

She surfaces, runs her hand through her hair, shakes out her upper body. Completely wet she is another person, and as she limbers up feels herself stretching supple and self-assured. The old ladies notice and scuttle to the side. She throws you one final glance, combining a look of cold-water agony with one more distant. You feel yourself reacting, putting the book away and coming into the open. You are already beginning to stare.

However, she can't catch you at it; she's taken out her contact lenses and can barely see you, or anything else. After pushing off her progress drifts sidewards until she catches blurry sight of the lane markers on the pool bottom. Then it's like the starter's gun has gone, and her throttle roars open.

She's into the crawl, one of her competition strokes, and now you are staring hard, as what you've only ever known as large and at loggerheads suddenly is surging slick and streamlined. Her stroke is machinery, fluid looping arms displacing the exact amount of water with each rotation. Her legs scissor up resistance with a sure sensuousness that goes straight to your groin. She passes the lengths man, a flailing moth in her wake. He pulls up short, spluttering, turns to say something, but she's gone.

At the far end she executes a deft flip turn, something she'd moaned all the way to the pool she couldn't do anymore. (You flatter yourself thinking she's done it for you, that she feels you up there cheering her on.) Her progress shows no sign of flagging, the machinery has settled into the seemingly effortless lope of the champion. You worry that she isn't going to see the wall but, like a braking machine, her arm flicks out, makes contact, and she stops. Waves gently bob her up against the run-off trough.

She's looking vacantly at you, the way she did that day in the country when you'd finally cast off those adolescent shackles and gone over and said hello. She was standing on the steps of the rambling halfway house she was living in at the time. She didn't remember you. She was wearing long sleeves on one of the year's hottest days. She was fleshier than you recalled, time having outstripped precocity. Yet her eyes carried a famished look, as though the weight she'd put on had only increased some private craving. The air around her still crackled with defiance, and when, in an attempt to establish both camaraderie and her social situation, you asked her if anybody from home ever came to visit she answered, *yes my parents tonight*, so razor sharp you half-wished for an old school locker to dive into. But then you remembered your age (and oh, what a relief *that* was) and asked her out for the following day.

(When she smiled and purred, why not? you wanted to phone all your old school friends and shout *so there!* Some things age can only mask.)

Her look has now widened – though not towards you or anyone in particular. She's resting her chin on the poolside, body splayed behind her like a bullfrog. *Blind as a bat* you cluck, and wave hard until she does see you. She tugs at the corner of her eye to bring you into focus, then waves back. Her face is flushed exertion red; you can see her blotchy cleavage heaving. Her smile is again gigantic – her famous axolotl grin, an expression coined by you after stopping by her place one day and meeting the grin's original owners, a pair of albino-pink salamanders with mouths wrapping halfway around their heads. Their aquarium is the cornerstone of an alphabet of animals she keeps with childlike devotion. 'Axolotls,' she'd lectured you, 'abhor the land. They've got arms and legs and everything, but they want no part of it. They were born for water.' Seen through the aquarium glass their grins looked even bigger. 'They're supposed to grow up eventually. Join the rest of the family on dry land. But most of them never do. They just hang around for ever underwater, living, mating, dying. Grinning all the time. Answerable to nobody except themselves.' (Her parents had forbidden pets in the house on the grounds that they'd only die, which would upset her, which would upset her parents. From time to time they suggested she bring home a little schoolfriend instead. She didn't.)

After a few minutes' rest she signals you with a series of fluttering motions. She's going to try her old primary competitive stroke, the butterfly. You give her the thumbs-up and fan an imaginary pennant. She's told you about swimming butterfly, an exhaustingly difficult stroke – how some days she couldn't lift her arms over her head after practice, how right from the start her coach drove her all around the country for worthwhile competition and training, how for a while she was winning everything in sight. How gratifying it felt. How it should have paid off; this was to be her moment of girlhood glory. Her Olympic event.

She pushes off again and you notice everyone's eyes are glued to her. Where her crawl was measured machinery her butterfly is all aqueous emoting: she throws herself at the water, is beaten down by it, rises up and shakes it off only to throw herself at it again. You watch her hair lashing like a coachman's crop at her neck, half-expecting blood. You notice the lifeguard: he's stopped twirling his whistle and is angling towards her, his face wide with admiring shock. Your reaction is one of vicarious pride; a chest-swell of association. Gratification is catching.

She makes another deft turn and is on the bell lap back to you. You forget yourself, throw down your book and double-jump the steps to the balcony. You teeter over the railing and wave frantically thinking she must see me, she *must* see me. The slamming, pungent sounds of flesh against water rush past you on their way up to the roof. She *must* . . .

Down the final stretch and her head is snapping back in a gasp of exhalation and then her eyes are straining straight at
– through –
you. For it is in that second, and it is only a second, that you know she doesn't; she is thirteen, hopeful, vulnerable – *winning!* Her coach roaring from the poolside, her body

exploding with power and confidence and glee, her eyes scouring the bleachers, each time finding only strange faces, each time nearer achievement and adulation and acceptance seeing only strangers, strangers, strangers, until she once again locates, amid the cheering, those horrible two empty seats.

And she wants to give up but she's already won.

For she is a champion, and as she touches the wall you realize that that is precisely what you've been tailing, that champion's secret you've fallen for but can never know; which always absorbs the blows, the excesses the rest of her can't, yet still thrives and directs, reigning triumphant in the axolotl grin she's beaming at you.

Craving Ertia

I

You're thirty-one, too young for Nam nostalgia, too ornery for TV-familyness, too old to look sexy in cycling shorts. You're sojourning in Europe, supposedly looking for some answers the way all those 1920s types did but let's face it, you haven't been looking too hard for a long time, except at the miraculous diversity of the London pub. You may have had notions of writing a book or composing a symphony or singing in a band or going in for a spot of higher education. Ersatz bohemia as a last resort. But not even that – here you are on the dark side of thirty, ontologically inert, physically dazed and bleeding, stretched out on the sidewalk, your bike, pretzeled by brakes you were too lazy to adjust and an impatient taxi, inert beside you. What you really want is a tin cup. Your mother's been saying it for years, it's your life's refrain: this is what happens when you don't pay attention.

Answers you wanted in college, or at least you thought

you did: Truth. Sort of. Nothing too tricky. Which is how you muddled through, how no doubt you were expected to muddle through life – by not rocking the boat. By subtly craving inertia. Which you would've accomplished by now if it weren't for an impulsive postgraduate crush on craving ertia, a lust to grab the world by the poles and squeeze until life ran red. The ripeness of possibility! The enormity! Overnight those around you became tiresome – the previous generation, their much-fawned-over excesses, their growing-up in public, the fact that finally grown-up they were running things much the same as your own parents. Would Jane Fonda tell you that this is what happens when you don't pay attention? Of course she would. So off to London, leave the 1980s to stew in their own self-actualizing juices, revert to a simpler, more lucid culture where they had yet to invent the bathroom shower or the tape of the workout book.

Truth. Are you bitter? You're certainly not mild. That pub motif again. Mine's a pint of special, and a packet of plain crisps for dinner, ta. You've even started talking like a Brit. What are you doing here? You dried up soon after arriving; the 1980s dragged on for nine vapid years. The cab driver's looming over you, saying, 'Sorry mate but you were in me blind spot', and he's not going to do a thing more until the cops get here. 'Just to be on the safe side you understand' – nobody's going to have cause to sue *him*. And all you want is for him to get out of the sun – it's so rare that you feel the sun in this dank country, if you can at least bleed to death in its maternal warmth then you will have achieved something.

The squawk of your radio – naturally the only thing to escape unscathed – reminds you that in the eyes of some you're not dead yet. Your controller wants to know your whereabouts, why you haven't dropped in EC1 yet. You are a very large letdown to your controller, who took you on years ago solely because you were an American, and therefore a born go-getter and moneymaker, something England had grown to respect but still couldn't quite bring itself to emulate; yet something, in light of rustling market forces, the despatch company thought they wanted. (How then to tell them about the sinister CIA plot to ship all the Yank under- and non-achievers to England, where they would mate with the natives and produce a mutant shopkeeping strain, perfect for staffing the hotdog stands of an American-run Authentic Olde Englande Nationpark?) Your head is hurting, your legs are wobbly, your radio buzzing like a swarm of killer bees at your shoulder. A crowd is gathering. You really ought to call in (you really ought to be in bed), you click your talk button once, twice, thrice, but it's engaged and with your usual admirable American persistence you switch it off, slump back down on the curb and hang your head between your legs.

And wonder what your grandparents are doing right now. That's right — those two wizened wonderful big-hearted people, never done anybody wrong, spent the majority of near ninety years fretting about their family in that time-honored tradition of making things better for the kids and grandkids . . . Christ if you die here, now, in this situation it'll probably kill them. Grandchildren simply do not shuffle off before their elders. Before fulfilling their potential. Oh God, what can you possibly come up with in your final five minutes that will begin to do justice to their commitment? And worse, what if you live and end up with a family yourself, how can you ever make things better for (God forbid) your own children? By keeping them well away from bicycles for starters. No seriously, you've suddenly decided that this is important. Your grandparents have left you and all their grandchildren a substantial nest egg, they've entrusted you with the stability and ongoingness of the world. As they know it. As they've worked it. As they've made it.

What about the ozone layer?

Ah.

What about the elephant? And the great blue whale?

And where is the world going to dump the discards from all these accumulated generations of stability and ongoingness?

Now your head is really hurting. Bed presents itself as the only logical answer but your brain's opting for the soapbox. Adrenalin is a poison.

When you were a kid, right, ecology was fun. It was new, it was clubby, it allowed you to do things – muck around filthy rivers seeing who could carry off the most shopping carts and old TVs and used tires – that your parents never would have approved of under any other conditions. And with adult supervision, no less. The innocence of the movement matched your own – the novelty was the power. And now the novelty is extinct, along with the dapper green-and-white flag and attendant terminology (who says 'ecology' anymore?), the innocence desperately rehashed for a now necessary nostalgia machine, the whole movement polluted by its own horrible necessity.

Shame you can't think this clearly all the time.

Things are dying every day – species, regions, ecosystems (how proudly that word once tripped off your eleven-year-old tongue!), people. With your last gasping monoxide-rich breath you should be warning your fellow man, shouting to the Old Street roundabout that, like that beer commercial from your youth, you only go around once in life. Same with the planet. And why are we all so convinced with ongoingness when we so cheerfully slaughter the hope of it in the name of going on?

But you don't shout do you; you lean forward and place your head on the cool slick tarmac at the taxi's wheel. You're dried up. You're dying. Drive, you call to the driver, follow that train of thought. Several passers-by (who will in a few years contract cancer from chemicals dumped in the water to improve their quality of life) leap out from the pavement and haul you back. You are polite, you mutter thanks. You're a nice boy. They keep a strong grip on you none the less. Somebody goes off to phone an ambulance.

II

It's that old enormity that's really doing your head in, isn't it? It's the reason why you're not paying attention – because being a good American, you were worried about said quality of life for future generations, and unfortunately right here in the middle of Clerkenwell Road the problem just kept unfolding and unfolding, link upon sickening link, dependency upon disintegrating dependency, getting bigger and bigger until the only solution (in a head also occupied with the shortest distance between W1 and EC1 and the pub) was the wholesale eradication of the human race.

Which would include your grandparents.

Whereupon disaster struck.

That's it, isn't it?

Relax, kid, relax. You're just one person, remember? You can't solve all the world's problems in one ride. For the time being you should just be concerned with staying alive on the streets of London. You're doing the world the most good that way. Crave inertia. And remember not to litter, and put your trust in your leaders, they've been elected by the people, they'll take care of everything –

Sorry, that was just a test. You know, see if your reflexes are still working. Full marks to you. You can calm down now. Let go of his collar.

So. Does this mean that in the possibly final hours of your dried-up existence you're deciding that perhaps it's time to get wet behind the ears again?

Your timing always was appalling.

No, no – I mean yes, yes. Bully. Bully for you.

All right – have it your way. Yabba-dabba-do. Whatever.

And that no doubt's what all this craving ertia business was/is about. Motion, activity, will carry the day. Feel the burn . . . However, currently you're a bit, ah, run down, and can't figure where all that energy has gone. That's the real problem isn't it? As you get older everything gets heavier, and all you end up feeling is the weight. (That'll be the pub again.) Yet you still demand the truth, served up in the old – dare we say it – gimme-gimme-some vessel, but can't seem to connect on the direct action front. You know, letters, demos, rallies, catchy sloganeering – hell, Hyde Park's got a whole corner set aside for people like you. And you know about that, because you've stood in front of your bedsit mirror, mouth rabid with toothpaste, and imagined yourself out there, tintinnabulating, ringing out rationale. Men nodding, stroking their chins thoughtfully, women going slightly weak (postfeministically, of course), children looking up at them and asking 'Why aren't you like that?' Truth by the balls. And you'd open your mouth, indicate with your toothbrush: behold the Earth, the beloved, sweet, hard-done-by Earth, depository of our dreams, holdall of our history, our alpha and omega and . . .

. . . Toothpaste would dribble down your chest. Real sitcom stuff. And suddenly that would be all folks – your goodness you is that the time must dash – save the world later. Off pedalling furiously, already swearing at motorists, while spat toothpaste (chockful of God knows what scientific wonders) swirled merrily into the food chain.

Was it all too embarrassing?

Or just too much effort?

Never mind. That's just a worst case scenario. And anyway your teeth always were too skanky for it to be very accurate.

They are all still in there, aren't they? . . . No, I'm not going to shut up. I'm your fault. You brought me out of the pit, to convince yourself that if you're still thinking, you can't be dead. Well I quite like it up here. Nice and sunny. No wonder you get so upset, it's actually not bad in the middle of Clerkenwell Road. I can even see the dome of St Paul's. Very nice against that royal blue sky. Imagine this view with everybody dragging themselves through it, 'limbs shaped like questions/in their odd twist' (that's right, your favorite Stephen Spender what-a-bitch-life-is line), thanks to ozone cancer or additive cancer or something-in-the-water cancer or just plain fagged-out exhaustion from trying to go on in a world they've irrevocably done their bit to stop. St Paul's dwarfed behind a K2 of shopping carts, old TVs and used tires. And bodies . . .

Hey, worst case scenario, remember? Worst case scenario – stop hitting yourself!

After all, it's not the end of the world, right?

Ah, the ambulance siren.

You'll soon be OK. Probably just superficial. Couple of hours, overnight at the most. Just to keep an eye on you – can't have you running around saving the world with a bump like that on your noggin, can we? Not good for PR. You Americans think you can do everything, immediately. Results. Well you can't.

III

Well, now that you're in the capable hands of the Knights of St John I suppose it's time for me to go below. Oh well. See if they can take the bike along too – maybe you can sell it to Young Unknowns as found art. You know, 'a powerful statement reflecting the twisted and inoperable framework of postindustrial excess.' Pays the bills while you're sick and hurt and can't work. Very Mutual of Omaha.

OK, OK, I'm going. But don't worry, we'll be talking again. Frequently. And in the meantime you might as well get started; I mean if you're going to live, that is. If you're still craving ertia. I suggest your mother as role model; if the world were run by mothers instead of politicians things would probably be much better. Certainly less scary. So go on, lean over to the nice ambulance man, waggle your finger admonishingly and say: 'This is what happens when you don't pay attention.'